"First, I'm going to give you a little advice," Aaron began. "Never, ever tell Mom you're playing football. That was a mistake you cannot repeat."

"Okay, don't tell Mom about football. Got it. What is the League of Pain?"

"It's our own league," Aaron explained. "We play in the park and we make our own rules. And nobody knows about it except the people who play in it."

"Who plays in it?" I asked.

"Some people you know and some people you don't know," Aaron answered.

"Can I play?"

"You can watch. That's all I can promise."

"When?"

"Our first game is at noon on the first Monday of summer vacation."

"That's the first day of golf camp," I said.

Aaron shrugged. "That's your problem."

That was my problem, but I had already made up my mind that I was not going to golf camp. *I* was going to choose what I did this summer, not Mom or Dad.

THE LEAGUE

Thatcher Heldring

A Yearling Book

Text copyright © 2013 by Thatcher Heldring
Cover photograph copyright © 2013 by Lisette Le Bon/SuperStock

Visit us on the Web! randomhousekids.com

Educators and librarians, for a variety of teaching tools, visit us at
RHTeachersLibrarians.com

The Library of Congress has cataloged the hardcover edition of this work as follows:
Heldring, Thatcher.
The league / Thatcher Heldring. — 1st ed.
p. cm.
Summary: Fourteen-year-old Wyatt, hoping to impress a girl and ward
off a bully, decides to join his older brother's summer football league, "The League
of Pain," against the advice of his parents, who think golf is the right sport for him.
ISBN 978-0-385-74181-1 (hc : alk. paper) —
ISBN 978-0-375-99025-0 (glb : alk. paper) — ISBN 978-0-375-98713-7 (ebook)
[1. Self-perception—Fiction. 2. Interpersonal relations—Fiction. 3. Bullies—Fiction.
4. Football—Fiction. 5. Golf—Fiction. 6. Family life—Fiction.] I. Title.
PZ7.H3734Le 2013
[Fic]—dc23
2012035296

ISBN 978-0-385-74182-8 (pbk.)

Printed in the United States of America

10 9 8 7 6 5 4 3 2 1

First Yearling Edition 2015

For big, tough Peter

CHAPTER ONE

"What do you want to see?" I asked Evan outside the movie theater. My mom had just driven away, and Evan's dad was going to pick us up afterward.

Evan lived next door and was in eighth grade like me, but she went to a different school. She had brown eyes, long dark hair in braids that fell just below her shoulders, and dimples that came out of nowhere whenever she smiled. Her feet had tan lines from the flip-flops she had been wearing since the sun came out in late March. Now it was late May, which meant summer vacation would begin in less than a month.

"Whatever," she said. "As long as it isn't rated R, sold out, or something I've already seen."

Evan was wearing baggy gym shorts and a long-sleeved T-shirt, which was typical since she was always coming from or going to some practice—today it was lacrosse. She bit her lower lip as she stared at the list of movies. I always liked the way her nose scrunched up when she did that.

"And nothing with *love* in the title," I added.

"Or anything longer than two hours," said Evan. "I need to be home by six o'clock so I can eat dinner before lacrosse practice."

That left only one choice: a baseball movie. I'd been wanting to see it anyway. I was on a baseball team this spring. I'd chosen baseball because I thought it might get Dad off my back about playing golf. He had been pushing me to get better so we could play together more often.

"How about *Swing and a Miss*?" I asked.

"Yeah, okay, I guess. But get ready to pay up if I don't like it."

That was the deal Evan and I had. Whoever picked the movie had to buy the other person's ticket if the movie stank. Luckily Mom and Dad gave me money for every A on my report card. I'd earned enough to fill up a jumbo peanut butter container I kept on my desk.

"It can't be worse than *Surf's Up*," I said while we were waiting in line.

Evan patted her heart twice. "That was my bad."

It was my turn at the ticket window. "One for *Swing and a Miss,* please," I said, passing my money through the slot to the woman in the booth.

"Child or adult?" the woman asked.

"Adult," I said, grinding my teeth. I wanted to put my face up against the glass and yell, *Can't you see I'm in the eighth grade!*

The woman looked surprised as she counted out my change. "How old are you?"

"Fourteen." I hated these conversations. I wished I looked my age. Knowing Evan was standing right behind me didn't help.

I held out my hand and took the money from the woman.

"You look younger," she said.

"Thanks," I said, even though it wasn't a compliment.

Evan didn't say anything as we went inside the lobby. Maybe she hadn't heard my conversation with the woman in the ticket booth. Still, I just wanted to get to the dark theater, where nobody could see me.

At the snack bar, I got a small bucket of popcorn and a soda. "Are you getting anything?" I asked her.

Evan pointed at the bucket. "Can I just share with you?"

"You don't want to get your own? This is a small."

Evan tilted her head and fluttered her eyelashes. "Wyatt, you're supposed to share your popcorn when you bring a girl to the movies."

I felt my face turn red. "You mean like a date?"

I had never been on a date with a girl, but if I ever went on one, I hoped it would be with Evan.

"I wish this was a date, buddy," said Evan. "I'd make you buy me a jumbo bucket and a large soda and some gummy bears. Then I'd throw up all over you."

"If you did that, I'd make you buy me a new shirt."

"Lucky for you we're just friends," Evan said.

I am lucky, I told myself as we left the concession area. *I am at the movies with Evan Robinson, and nobody else can say that.*

We had some time to kill before the movie, so we found a free table in the café above the lobby. We could see all the people below coming in and out of the theater. On the wall next to us were posters for upcoming summer movies.

Evan gasped and pointed to a poster for *The All-Star.* There was a girl in a football uniform holding a helmet. "I totally want to see that," she told me. "Opening day, we have to be first in line."

"What about *Dr. Pirate*? That looks hilarious. Do you think he operates on people with the hook?"

Evan laughed. "Now I have to know."

"And *Invasion Earth Two Three-D*," I said. "We have to see that too."

Suddenly Evan kicked me under the table. "Wyatt, check it out!" she whispered, even though it was too loud in the café to hear other people's conversations. "It's Brian Braun." She pointed to a guy in the lobby wearing cargo shorts, a dark green T-shirt, and a backward baseball cap.

"Brian Brian?"

"Brian *Braun*," said Evan. "He's basically the best quarterback ever from Pilchuck. He broke like a million passing records last season. He could probably go pro."

I watched as Brian led his friends across the lobby to the theater entrance, where he greeted the ticket taker by slapping his hand. He gestured to the pack behind him, and the guy let them all pass without handing over any tickets.

"He didn't even pay," I said, becoming instantly jealous of Brian Braun. He was tall. He had a lot of friends. He got into movies for free. And Evan was paying attention to him.

"That's what being good at football gets you," Evan said. She jumped up like a cheerleader. "Come on, let's go down there."

"You want to talk to him?"

"I hope I don't make a fool of myself."

Too late, I thought, following Evan to the lobby. She turned to me as we hustled down the stairs.

"If we see him, I'll tell him you're my little brother."

"Gee, thanks."

Evan reached the bottom of the stairs. "Sorry, but you know he'll never believe we're twins." She stood on the tips of her toes but didn't see him.

"You could always tell him you're adopted," I said as we went to the theater to get seats. I was happy Brian had vanished, but as we sat down, I knew that as far as Evan was concerned, he might as well have been sitting next to us.

Evan sighed. "I can't get him out of my mind."

"It's only been five minutes."

Evan opened her eyes wide. "Can you believe we'll be at the same school in three months?"

Wow, I thought. *I guess I'm not the only one looking forward to walking down the hallway together.* "Actually, it's more like two and a half."

"Even better," Evan said. "I hope my locker is close to his. No, I take that back. I hope it isn't. Or maybe close, but not too close." Then she leaned over, reaching into my bucket of popcorn. "May I?" she asked, already feeding herself a handful.

"Just don't eat too much and barf on my shirt," I said, feeling a bit sick to my stomach knowing that Evan would rather be sitting next to Brian than me.

She reached over and pinched the sleeve of my T-shirt. "That wouldn't cost me much," she said. "Probably less than the bucket of popcorn. Unless you put on something nice, like for a date."

"I don't have anything nice except a suit."

Evan laughed. "If you ever go on a date, you have to promise me you'll wear a suit."

"Deal," I whispered as the movie started. "But only if you promise to stuff yourself and barf."

"Pinky swear," Evan whispered back. She held out her right pinky and curled it around my left one. The moment lasted only a few seconds before Evan let go to drive her hand into my bucket of popcorn.

About ten minutes into the movie, I knew Evan was going to make me pay for her ticket. *Swing and a Miss* had nothing to do with a strikeout. The main character was named Swing, and Miss was the daughter he never knew who showed up at his house one day. The whole movie was about him taking her shopping and her teaching him how to dance. They never played baseball.

"Nice pick, Wyatt," Evan whispered.

• • •

After the movie, Evan and I waited in front of the theater for her dad. I was still blinking my eyes from the late-afternoon sunshine after the dark theater when Evan elbowed me in the ribs and started rifling through her pockets.

"What?" I asked. "Is your dad here?"

She looked over at me. "Quick," she said. "Give me some garbage."

"Why?"

She pointed to a group of people standing not far from an overflowing trash can. One of them was Brian Braun. "I need something to throw away," Evan pleaded.

"What's that going to do?"

"I don't know," Evan replied impatiently. "Maybe he'll think I'm a good citizen."

"Maybe he'll think you work here," I replied, handing Evan a stick of gum.

"Ha, ha. Thanks." Evan took the gum, popped it into her mouth, then spit it into the wrapper as she made her way over toward Brian. When she got to the trash can, she dropped the gum inside, but Brian still hadn't noticed her. Instead of walking back like a normal person, Evan reached into the can, picked up the gum, which had been sitting at the top, and tossed it in again. That didn't work either. Evan looked over at me. I shook my head. She was just going back in for the gum when a woman in a hurry walked by, tossing a cup into the can and splattering Evan.

She came back smelling like coffee.

"I'm not giving up," she said.

"What's the big deal about him?" I asked.

"I don't know," Evan said. "He's just . . . I can't think of the word."

Her eyes stayed glued on Brian as he jumped into the back of a Jeep with his friends and sped away. *That's what being good at football gets you,* I thought, watching Evan watch Brian drive off.

I hoped it was the last time we'd see Brian Braun at the cineplex. Little did I know, I'd have bigger problems this summer than Brian Braun.

CHAPTER TWO

There was still plenty of daylight left when I got home from the movies. Mom was in the kitchen helping my sister, Kate, with long division and checking her email. She was an emergency-room nurse, which meant she saw a lot of gross injuries, like people with bleeding heads and arms twisted in the wrong direction. I figured Dad had already left on his next business trip. He was a consultant, which meant he traveled all the time. Some weeks he'd leave Sunday evening and be gone until Thursday.

Kate was eleven, three years younger than me, but she and I were almost the same height. She had blond hair like Mom and Aaron. I got Dad's dark brown hair, which I wore short.

"Where's Aaron?" I asked.

"He's in the backyard," Mom answered. "He should be cutting the grass."

"Because he stole Mom's money," added Kate, laying her pencil on the table.

Pushing the pencil back to Kate, Mom said, "He didn't steal the money, sweetie. He just misspent it."

A week ago, Mom had given Aaron money to take me and Kate to her school carnival. She said it was a chance for Kate to spend more time with us boys, but really I think she was just looking for an excuse to get out of going to the carnival herself.

Ignoring the pencil by her right hand, Kate said, "All I know is he has to cut the grass or he can't use the car tonight. He's supposed to drive Sara Morelli to River Tunes. Otherwise she's probably going to break up with him." Kate went back to her long division. "He deserves it," she said to herself.

Sara Morelli was Aaron's girlfriend, and River Tunes was a free concert by the water.

"Kate, focus on your math," said Mom. "You need to do well on this test."

Kate got pretty good grades, but she was having a hard time with math. Mom had promised to buy her a set of golf clubs if she got at least a B on her end-of-the-year test. Not what I would have asked for, but Kate really liked golf.

11

Turning her attention back to me, Mom asked, "How was the movie, Wyatt?"

"Let's just say there won't be a sequel," I said, grabbing a granola bar from a jar on the kitchen counter.

Putting her pencil down again, Kate asked Mom, "How come everyone in this family gets to go somewhere fun except me?"

"What do you mean?" Mom asked.

"Wyatt went to a movie. Aaron is going to River Tunes. But does anybody take me? Noooo. Because I'm Kate Parker, the girl the whole world ignores."

"Did you say something?" I asked, munching on the granola bar as I pushed open the back door.

"Ha, ha," said Kate, glaring at me.

On the back porch, I opened the storage bin and dug through a pile of mitts and racquets until I found the football Dad gave Aaron when he turned thirteen. The next year, Aaron made the freshman team at Pilchuck High School. That was two years ago. Mom thought it was dangerous, but Dad said it taught Aaron discipline. This year, Aaron was going to try out for varsity.

At the moment, Aaron was lying faceup in the long grass. Nearby was the lawn mower, standing idle with a short strip of cut grass in its wake. Beyond that was a tire swing hanging from the limb of the maple tree that shaded our whole yard.

"Mom says get to work."

Aaron looked over without getting up. "Tell her I'm taking a break."

"From what? You cut like five feet of grass."

"It's harder than it looks. The grass is wet."

I glanced down at the football I was holding. I tossed it a few times up into the air, hoping Aaron would see, but he had gone back to his break. "As long as you're not working, do you want to play football?" I asked.

"With who?"

"Me."

"Don't make me laugh."

"I know how to play football."

"You don't even know how to throw a football."

"I'll cut the grass for you."

Aaron opened one eye. "You'll cut the grass if I play football with you?"

I nodded.

"You get ten minutes," said Aaron, pushing himself to his feet.

"Fifteen," I replied.

Aaron stretched and rubbed his chin. "Twelve. I need time to shower and shave."

When Aaron was ready, I spread my fingers out across the laces of the football and held it up. "Is this right?" I asked.

"Sure," he said.

I brought my arm back and let it fly. The ball wobbled, landing halfway between me and Aaron.

"You've got to be kidding," Aaron grumbled as he shuffled over to the football. He tossed back a tight spiral that bounced off my hands.

"Hallelujah," Aaron said when I threw the next ball all the way to him.

Aaron's next pass was also perfect, spinning so fast it was impossible to tell by the white stripes if the football was even moving.

"How do you do that?" I asked.

"It can't be taught," Aaron answered.

"Come on," I said. "You said you'd teach me."

"I said I'd throw the ball around with you. I never said I'd teach you anything," Aaron said, sniffing his armpit. "Oh man," he muttered. "I stink. I gotta hit the shower." Gesturing to the lawn, he added, "Don't forget to bag the clippings."

"That wasn't twelve minutes," I said. "That's a breach of contract."

"Sue me," Aaron shot back, heading inside. "Aim for the tire swing if you want a target," he added before disappearing into the house.

I didn't really feel like mowing the lawn for Aaron, so I started throwing the football at the tire swing. My first five passes missed the tire completely. My sixth bounced off the top of the rubber. But by the tenth throw, it sailed through.

"Wyatt, what are you doing?" asked Dad, walking toward me in his work clothes.

"Just practicing," I said, startled.

"Sorry, kiddo, didn't mean to scare you."

"That's okay. I just didn't know you were home."

"Just got here," he said, taking the football in his hands. "You're practicing football?" Dad sounded like he didn't quite believe me.

"Kinda," I said.

"Any special reason?" Dad asked.

"Not really."

Dad walked over to me. "Football is a tough sport, kiddo. It's not for everyone."

"Aaron plays."

"And he takes a beating."

I stared back at Dad, hoping he would offer to play catch. "How about we play nine after school tomorrow?" he asked. "We'll grab Jim and Francis and make it a foursome."

Francis was my best friend and Jim was his dad. The four of us had been golfing together for a few years. I was getting pretty good, but I wasn't sure it was the sport for me. Mom and Dad had signed me up for two weeks of golf camp this summer. Kate was going too, but she was actually excited about it.

"Okay," I said. "I guess."

I must have sounded disappointed, because Dad patted me on the back. "Trust me," he said. "I'm doing you a favor. Football is no picnic. Ask your brother about wind sprints in full gear under the August sun."

"Can I keep throwing?"

"Sure," said Dad, smiling. "In fact, I'll play catch with you."

Dad and I tossed the football back and forth until it got dark. My right arm was aching by the time I went inside. Later, as the burn faded, I flexed my biceps and wondered if I could ever look like Brian Braun, or if I could get strong enough to throw a football so hard it would bounce off someone's hands. That night, I took the football to my room. The golf outing tomorrow was the furthest thing from my mind.

CHAPTER THREE

The clock was ticking down fast and I had to cover thirty yards of hallway before reaching safety. I didn't look back, but I knew he was behind me somewhere. Spencer Randle was lumpy, but he could move. I raced through the crowded hallway, zigging and zagging around anyone who got in my way. Up ahead I could see Francis waiting in front of Mr. Leland's classroom. He was holding his lunch bag in one hand and waving me in with the other.

I made it to the door just as the bell rang.

"Any sign of him?" Francis asked as he looked around nervously.

I knew he meant Spencer, the biggest bully in

school. When Francis and I were in second grade, Spencer was in fourth. Now we were in the same grade. Spencer had shaggy hair, flabby arms, and meaty hands. As far as I could tell, he didn't own a single shirt with sleeves. The last time I'd seen him, about thirty seconds earlier by the drinking fountain, he was wearing a football jersey with the arms cut off.

"All clear," I said. "For now. Let's go inside. During gym class this morning I heard him tell Troy Bunyon he had something to take care of during lunch."

"Oh man," said Francis as he knocked on the door. "I'm glad we'll be in here."

A while back, Francis and I started eating lunch in Mr. Leland's classroom. We'd help him out by wiping down his whiteboard or organizing his bookshelves, and he'd let us hang out until it was time to go back to class.

We were just about to go inside when Mr. Leland opened his door. "Sorry, boys," he said. "I have a parent meeting today. You'll have to find somewhere else to eat lunch."

"We'll be quiet," I promised. "And anything we overhear would never leave your room. I swear."

"I'm sure I can trust you, Wyatt. You weren't voted school citizen of the year for nothing." Mr. Leland smiled. "But it wouldn't be right. You understand?"

"We'll label every bone on your skeletons," Francis pleaded. "We'll clean your microscopes for a week."

"Sorry," Mr. Leland said, starting to push the door closed.

"A month!" I added.

"School will be over in a month," Mr. Leland replied. "Try something new. It's a big world out there. Go enjoy it."

"But I like it in here," I said.

"Shoo."

Then the door closed in our faces.

"Where do you want to go?" asked Francis. "We could try the cafeteria."

"No thanks. The last time we ate in there, Spencer poured a carton of milk on my head. Remember?"

Francis pushed his light brown hair away from his eyes. "How could I forget? It was my milk."

"How about the playground?" I asked. The playground was really for the elementary school kids next door, but we were allowed to go there as long as we didn't leave school grounds.

Francis nodded. "Wide open, good sightlines, plenty of places to run if we have to. I guess it'll have to do."

So we went outside.

Francis and I sat on opposite sides of the merry-go-round so we could see in all directions. We were both using our feet to spin slowly in a circle while we ate our lunches.

Not far away, on the grassy area, McKlusky and Raj were tossing a football back and forth. McKlusky was on the same rec-league baseball team as me. He was one of the tallest kids in our school. If Francis stood on my shoulders we still wouldn't be as tall as McKlusky.

"Football is stupid," Francis said. "It's just physics. If you're bigger, you win."

"I don't think it's that simple," I said, unwrapping my sandwich.

"Trust me," said Francis. "It is."

I didn't argue with Francis. He'd never admit he was wrong anyway.

I watched from the merry-go-round as McKlusky lobbed a high pass that sailed just over Raj's hands. "Nice catch," I heard McKlusky say.

"How am I supposed to reach that?" Raj asked, annoyed. "Do I look like I have a ladder? I don't have stilts like you."

"Stilts," McKlusky said. "I like that. Call me Stilts."

"Don't even try it," Raj replied, picking up the football. "Nobody is going to call you Stilts."

I ate my sandwich and wondered what it would be like to play football. Would I be any good or would I get totaled the minute I stepped onto the field? Could I take a beating?

"I'd rather play a sport that requires some skill," Francis said a minute later. "Like golf."

I was finishing my sandwich when Francis got up from the merry-go-round and walked over to the garbage can. On his way back, he was facing the school. He suddenly froze. "Oh, great," he said. "It's Spencer, and he's closing in fast."

The merry-go-round slowed to a stop, and now I could see Spencer too, crossing the open space between the school and us like an elephant.

I kept chewing the last bite of my sandwich. I knew what I had to do: avoid eye contact, make no sudden moves, and most important of all, *say nothing*. That was how to survive an encounter with Spencer Randle.

I kept glancing casually in Spencer's direction, ready to run for my life if I had to.

Spencer was making his way down the path that led from the school building past the playground and out to Boardman Street. He stopped a few feet away from us. "What's up, dorks?" he asked.

"We're just eating our lunches," Francis said.

"Good for you," said Spencer, coming over to the

merry-go-round. "Don't you losers want to know where I'm going?" He said it like it was a big secret.

"Not really," Francis answered.

Spencer fixed his evil eyes on me. "You got something to say, Wyatt *Twerp*?" he asked.

"Not me," I said.

"Good. Keep it that way."

I watched nervously as Spencer leaned forward and grabbed one of the merry-go-round bars. I made a fist in case I needed to defend myself, but I knew if it came to that, it would be useless. I was no match for Spencer Randle in a fight. I was a puny little runt with chicken legs and no muscles, and my only hope was to run as fast as my chicken legs could carry me.

"I'm going to Pilchuck Market," Spencer said, looking over his shoulder. "For a corn dog."

"Sounds good," said Francis.

"Corn dogs aren't good," said Spencer as he let go of the bar. "They're awesome. They taste awesome, they come on an awesome stick, and they're awesome healthy because of the corn."

"I don't think that's actually corn," I said before I could stop myself.

Spencer turned around. "What did you say?" he asked.

"Nothing. I didn't say anything."

"That's funny," said Spencer. "I thought I heard

you say you wanted to give me some money for my corn dog."

"Uh-uh," I said, praying that a teacher would appear.

Spencer put his face right up to mine. "Either you said you wanted to give me some money or you said I didn't know what corn dogs were made out of, which would mean I was stupid. So which is it? Do you want to give me some money or do you think I'm stupid?"

Kicking myself for opening my mouth, I stood up and reached into my pockets. Spencer held out his hand while I gave him everything I had: a dollar bill, a quarter, and two pennies.

"Thanks, wimp," said Spencer, dropping the pennies on the ground. "Keep the change." Then he used his foot to shove the merry-go-round hard enough to make Francis lose his balance. "I'm outta here," he said as we spun slowly in a circle. "Don't try to follow me."

"Enjoy your corn dog," Francis called.

"It's not even for me. It's for a girl. Do you know what that is? Probably not." He laughed. "Oh, by the way, if you tell anyone where I am, I'll smash your brains in." Those were his last words. We watched him disappear around the bushes behind the playground and then he was out of sight.

"I hope he gets busted by Principal Groton and has to go to summer school," I said.

"Who cares what Spencer does this summer?" Francis said. "I'm pretty sure he won't be at the golf club. They wouldn't let a thug like him past the front gate."

That was one good thing about golf camp, I thought. Spencer and his tank tops would not be welcome at the Pilchuck Golf and Tennis Club. "I bet he could hit the ball a mile, though," I said.

"Speaking of hitting balls, we're on for golf after school today, right?" Francis asked. "I wonder if we'll have time to play eighteen."

"I think nine is enough," I replied. "I have two tests this week."

"Okay, you're right," Francis agreed. "We'll have all summer to play golf."

McKlusky and Raj came jogging over from the grassy area where they'd been throwing the football. "We saw the whole thing," said McKlusky. "How much did he get?"

"A dollar and twenty-five cents," I said, picking up the two pennies Spencer had dropped.

"You'll never see that money again."

Not unless I get a lot bigger, stronger, and braver in a hurry, I thought. And that wasn't going to happen hanging around a golf course with Francis. I had to do something dramatic that would show Spencer I wasn't afraid of him and make Evan think I was a man like Brian Braun.

• • •

It was drizzling when we reached the ninth hole, the last we'd play that day. My ball was lying in the tall grass about six feet from the green. I gave the ball a gentle tap with my chipper, getting underneath just enough to lift it over the grass. The ball landed softly on the green and picked up speed as it changed direction at the top of the hill.

"Looking good, Wyatt!" Dad called.

"Get in there!" Jim shouted.

"Find the hole," Francis said.

Now the ball was headed straight for the hole and it wasn't slowing down. I watched without blinking as it rolled right on top of the hole, hit the back rim, rattled around, and dropped in.

Dad put his arm around me. "That's one to remember, Wyatt," he said. "I've never hit a shot like that."

"I got lucky," I said, retrieving my ball from the hole.

"Luck?" Dad said, following me back to the cart. "Luck had nothing to do with that. You're a good golfer, Wyatt. Give yourself some credit."

I knew I had hit a great shot, but something weird was happening. The more excited Dad became about me and golf, the more I wanted to be anywhere else, doing anything else. Golf was the sport Dad had chosen, and I didn't like having decisions made for me. A round of golf now and then was okay, but two whole weeks of golf camp was another story. Especially when there were so many other sports I could be good at. Like football.

I stuffed the chipper in with the rest of my clubs and lifted my bag onto the cart. "Dad, it was no big deal," I said. "Can we just go?"

"Can you believe how humble this kid is?" Dad asked Jim as he sat behind the wheel of the cart.

"I guess you'll have to do all the bragging when you win the father-son tournament," Jim said with a smile.

"What did he say?" I asked as Dad drove us back to the clubhouse.

"I was going to surprise you later, but I guess the cat is out of the bag. I signed us up for the father-son tournament over the Fourth of July weekend, right after golf camp."

"Why did you do that?"

"Because I think it'll be fun."

"No, why did you do that without asking me?"

"I wanted to surprise you."

"Well, congratulations. I'm surprised."

"Cut it out, Wyatt. I don't like you talking to me like that. I want you to keep an open mind about the tournament. I think by July you'll be really glad I signed us up."

I didn't see that happening. As far as I was concerned at that moment, there was zero chance I would ever be glad Dad had signed me up for that tournament. I doubted Evan would be cuckoo over Brian Braun if he was the best golfer in Pilchuck. I wondered if Brian Braun's parents entered him in tournaments without asking.

CHAPTER FOUR

I was alone at my locker on Tuesday morning when Principal Groton walked up to me.

"Wyatt, did I see you go outside for lunch yesterday?" he asked. He sounded like he had something on his mind.

"We were at the playground the whole time," I said. "We didn't go anywhere else. It was Mr. Leland's idea."

Mr. Groton put his hand on my shoulder. "Relax. I know you didn't do anything wrong. I'm asking about Spencer Randle. I saw him leave the building and I thought you might have seen where he went."

I didn't say anything.

Mr. Groton fixed his eyes on me. "Did you see Spencer?" he asked.

I nodded.

"Was he outside?"

"Yes."

"Did you see where he went?"

"I'm not sure," I said. Technically, I hadn't seen where Spencer had gone. If Mr. Groton had walked away after that, I would have been in the clear. But instead he asked me one more question, and there was no way to avoid answering it without lying.

"Did he tell you where he was going?" Mr. Groton inquired as packs of kids swept by.

"Yes, he told me where he was going," I said, being sure not to reveal any more than I had to. "Can I go now?"

"Where did he say he was going, Wyatt? I promise anything you tell me will remain confidential."

"He said he was going to Pilchuck Market," I told Mr. Groton. "For a corn dog. But I didn't actually see him go, so he might have been making it all up."

Mr. Groton nodded and tightened his lips. "Thank you, Wyatt. Thank you for always telling the truth. I'll take it from here." He turned and quickly walked down the hallway.

I closed my locker. My heart was pounding. Maybe Mr. Groton would uphold his promise to keep our

29

conversation confidential, but something was bothering me. I was afraid I had said too much.

Just then, Francis appeared through the crowd. "Wanna go to the driving range this afternoon?" he asked. "My dad is picking me up after school and we're going straight there. He can hit a ball three hundred yards with an iron. It's unreal."

"I don't think so," I said quietly.

"What's with you?"

"Mr. Groton just asked me if I knew where Spencer Randle went yesterday. Actually, his exact words were 'Did he tell you where he was going?' "

"What did you say?"

"What could I say? I told him Spencer was going to Pilchuck Market. But don't worry, Mr. Groton won't say how he found out."

"Don't you think Spencer will figure it out?" Francis asked, his voice shaking. "I mean, what if we were the only people he told?"

"Spencer's so dumb, I bet he forgot he even talked to us. He probably doesn't remember what he did yesterday."

"Guess again," said Francis, looking over my shoulder.

I turned to see Mr. Groton leading Spencer by the elbow toward the principal's office.

"That's not good," I said to Francis.

"You got that right," Francis agreed. "We need to begin evasive maneuvers *now*. First order of business: how are you getting home this afternoon? You cannot take your normal route."

"Don't freak out," I said. "It's only a problem if Spencer knows it was me who told Mr. Groton."

"I'm sure he'll figure it out," said Francis. "You think he went around the whole school telling people he was going to Pilchuck Market for a corn dog? I seriously doubt it."

He was right and I knew it. I leaned back against my locker in despair. "I'm sick of being scared all the time," I told Francis.

"Don't you remember what we learned in science?" Francis asked. "Fear is good for you. Like when a rabbit sees a hawk and hides without even thinking about it. That's what we need to do—hide."

"I'd rather be the hawk."

"Well, I'd rather have the power of invisibility, but since that's not going to happen, I think you should start planning a new route home."

On our way to class, I ran into McKlusky, who was coming from the direction of Mr. Groton's office. "I have something to tell you," he said in a rush. "It's about what happened outside. I'll call you tonight."

I couldn't wait.

My first class after lunch was earth science, and

Mr. Leland put on a movie about the Arctic tundra. As I watched it I thought, *I'd like to be on the Arctic tundra right now.* I tried to forget about Spencer Randle, but my heart was racing. He could be anywhere waiting for me. I felt helpless. For once I was glad Evan didn't go to my school. I could never let her see me like this.

Halfway through class, Roy Morelli leaned over the aisle between our desks. Roy and I were on the same baseball team. His sister was also my brother's girlfriend, which I guess made us kind of related. Roy was probably the best player and I was probably the worst, but he was nice to me, unlike some of the other guys on the Pirates. Baseball was the only team sport I had ever really played. I wished Mom and Dad would let me sign up for football, but I think they saw that as Aaron's sport.

"If you have to take a leak, just ask for a bathroom pass," said Roy.

"What?"

Roy pointed to the ground. "You're tapping your foot like you drank a gallon of water during lunch. I figured you had a full tank."

"Mr. Morelli," Mr. Leland called. "No talking during the film."

"Sorry, Mr. Leland," said Roy. "I was just asking Wyatt if he had any questions."

Mr. Leland held a finger up to his lips.

"This is so boring," Roy whispered. "You wanna play a game or something?"

Sure, I thought. *How about a few rounds of hide from Spencer Randle? If you win, you get to keep all your limbs.* I crossed my legs to stop my foot from tapping and focused on the screen. I just hoped McKlusky had good news.

• • •

"Wyatt, honey," said Mom at dinner that night. "You haven't eaten anything. Is everything okay?"

I looked up from my plate of lasagna. "I'm not really hungry," I said.

Before Mom could pry, Dad started grilling Aaron. "Have you found something to do this summer?" he asked. He'd been pestering him with the same question since the snow melted in February.

"I'm working on it," Aaron answered without making eye contact.

"Tell me the truth," said Dad. "There is no lying in this house."

Forcing himself to look at Dad, Aaron said, "I swear, I'm working on it. I have some good leads."

"You could work at the golf club," said Kate.

"Good one," said Aaron.

"You might think it's lame," Kate replied, "but I can't wait. Golf is my favorite sport."

"If you call hitting a little ball that isn't even moving a sport," said Aaron. "If you want a real sport, you should try football." Aaron looked at me. "Didn't you say you wanted to play?"

"Wyatt said that?" Mom asked.

Aaron nodded. "Yeah, he asked me to teach him."

"Never," Mom said. "No way. Not my baby."

"Don't call me a baby," I said to Mom.

"Sorry, sweetie," Mom replied, brushing the hair out of my eyes. "I guess I still look at you and see my little boy."

That was the problem. I was tired of everyone looking at me and seeing a baby, a twerp, or a child who couldn't get into a PG-13 movie.

"You're probably right," Aaron said. "He'd get slaughtered in a football game."

"Well, he won't have to worry about that on the golf course," Dad said.

"What's the point of playing a sport if there's no chance of anything bad happening?" I asked.

"Just because there's no physical risk doesn't mean it isn't challenging," Dad said. "I've been playing since I was your age and I'm still tested every time I play."

Mom grabbed my hand. "Honey, trust me, you

don't want to go looking for sports injuries. I've seen too many blown-out knees and broken bones. Golf is a sport you can play your whole life."

I thought about arguing, but there was no point. She was talking about the rest of my life when the only thing on my mind was this summer. Somehow, I had to get out of golf camp and the father-son tournament.

After dinner that night I studied for my history test in the basement. This was supposed to be our homework area, but Aaron was on the phone.

"Hold on," I heard him say. "Other line." He clicked the phone once, then said, "Yeah?" There was a pause.

I put down my pen. I thought it might be McKlusky. "Is it for me?" I asked hopefully.

Aaron shook his head at me. "Sorry, there's no Wyatt here," he told the person on the other end of the line. Then he clicked the phone again and said, "Sorry about that. Wrong number. What were you saying?"

"Hey," I said. "I'm right here."

"I never said that to her," Aaron was saying. "I wasn't even looking at her. Who did you hear that from? Hello? Hello?" He slammed the phone, picked it up, and began dialing again.

I stood a foot away. "I'm right here," I said again.

Aaron ignored me. "What did you say to Sara?" he asked. "She just hung up on me because she thinks I was looking at Lily. If I get dumped because of this, that would not be cool. Call me back."

Aaron clicked the phone off and threw it on the couch. He turned and looked at me. "Yeah?" he said.

"I need the phone."

"Am I on the phone?" he asked.

"No."

"Then stop whining and leave me alone. I have real problems." He pushed me out of the way and sat down at his desk. Flipping open his laptop, he slipped on his headphones. I could hear the music blasting anyway.

My fingers were shaking as I dialed McKlusky's number. He answered on the first ring.

"This is Stilts."

"What does Spencer know?" I asked.

"He knows someone told Mr. Groton that he went to Pilchuck Market. I heard Mr. Groton tell him that he had a confidential source."

"What else? Does he know who told?"

"He might."

"What do you mean he might? Does he or doesn't he?"

"I can't be sure. Mr. Groton closed his door. But I did hear Spencer talking to himself when he was walking out of the office."

"What was he saying?"

"It sounded like *Why did I go to Pilchuck Market?* But he might have said *I'm going to kill Wyatt Parker.*"

"So either Spencer Randle *definitely* wants to smash my face in or he *might* want to smash my face in. Is that what you're telling me?"

"Basically," McKlusky admitted. "Man, I'm not looking forward to high school very much."

I had to agree.

The next morning I asked Mom to drop me off at school. I told her I wanted to get there early so I could study for my science test, which was partly true. The test was in a few days and I wanted to be ready. More importantly, I wanted to get safely inside the building before Spencer showed up.

"Can you pick me up too?" I asked as I unbuckled myself.

"Wyatt, is everything all right?" asked Mom. "Does something hurt? Is that why you don't want to walk?"

"Nothing hurts," I said. *Not yet, anyway,* I thought.

Mom tousled my hair. "Then I'll see you here a little before three."

"Okay," I said, focusing on spotting Spencer.

I got out of the car slowly, scanning the drop-off area for any sign of trouble. All I saw was a line of cars and minivans and kids hanging out peacefully in front of the school. The sun was shining through a layer of morning clouds. It was safe.

"No sign of him yet," I told Francis when we were at our desks for first-period math.

The bell rang and Mr. Morales asked everyone to be quiet for the morning announcements, which came over the PA system. Sometimes Mr. Groton made them and other times it was a student. I had never done it, but everyone knew the microphone was in a small room next to the office.

That morning, the announcements began like always. There was a chime that meant someone was about to speak. Then we heard a screech. All the people around me looked up and some of them covered their ears. Next came a few seconds of static, and then a familiar voice.

"Attention, Pilchuck Middle School. This is a message for the spineless weasel who ratted on Spencer Randle. You know who you are. So you better run and hide, because I am going to spend the rest of the school year tracking you down, and when I find you I am going to turn your face into mashed potatoes and then feed it to you, and your snot will be the gravy. Thank you and have a good day. Oh, and corn dogs are awesome."

There was another screech and then silence.

I felt my palms begin to sweat.

"Oh man, I'd hate to be whoever he's talking about," I heard Ruben say in the back of the room.

"I'd switch schools," said Khalil.

A few rows up, I saw Valerie and Emily whispering and giggling.

"All right, all right," said Mr. Morales as he stood at the front of the class with his hands in the air. "I'm sure that was just a practical joke. Let's settle down and let Mr. Groton deal with it."

Personally, I thought Mr. Groton had done enough already.

CHAPTER FIVE

After I did my homework that evening, I went out to the back porch to read *Frankenstein* for school. The porch was cluttered with rakes and shovels and bicycle parts, and the boards were so weak they creaked, but it was my favorite place to get away from my family. I had been there only a few minutes when Evan showed up.

This happened most nights when it was warm. I'd come to the porch to read and Evan would join me. We'd hang out and throw pebbles in a bucket or play twenty questions or "would you rather" or just read books like we were in a library.

She was twirling a lacrosse stick as she came up

the porch steps, a few feet from where I was sitting in an old armchair. "Think fast," she said, thrusting the head of the stick in my direction.

I knew Evan would never bean me with a lacrosse ball at close range, but I flinched anyway.

"Chicken," she said.

"Rooster," I said back.

Evan settled into the seat next to me, laying the lacrosse stick in her lap as she perched her feet on an empty milk crate. "Shouldn't I be a hen?" she asked after a minute.

"Rooster sounds funnier," I said, trying to concentrate long enough to finish the chapter I was reading.

"Rooster," said Evan. "Rooster. Hen. Rooster. Yeah, I guess you're right. It is funnier." She pointed her stick at my book. "It's good, right? We had to read it at my school too. You'll never guess how it ends."

"Don't tell me," I said as I closed the book.

"Frankenstein dies," said Evan.

"Nice try. He was already dead. He can't re-die."

"You're thinking of the monster," said Evan. "Frankenstein is the name of the doctor. The monster is just called the 'monster.' "

"So the doctor dies?" I asked.

"No," she said with a smile. "I was lying about that."

I looked over at Evan, who was wiggling her tan

41

toes to the beat of the music coming from Aaron's room. "Can I just read the book, please?"

Evan lay back in the lawn chair while I tried to focus on the book. I had read less than a full page when the back door opened and Aaron appeared on the porch.

He looked at Evan first. "What's up?" he asked.

"Not much," Evan said. She sounded bored. I guess Aaron was no Brian Braun.

Then, without warning, Aaron kicked my chair so hard I fell sideways onto the porch. "Are you stupid?" he asked me.

I climbed back into the chair. "What are you talking about?"

"Why did you rat on Spencer Randle? That dude's gonna tear your arms off and beat you with them."

"I didn't rat on him. At least, I didn't mean to. It was a misunderstanding. How do you know about this, anyway?"

"I know someone who knows him." Aaron shook his head. "Man, he's gonna make you pay. I should offer to help."

"Really?" I said, surprised that Aaron cared. "Thanks a lot."

"Not you!" Aaron snapped. "Him."

"Why would you do that? I'm your brother!"

Evan wasn't saying anything. She was just watching me and Aaron go back and forth.

"You dishonored the family," Aaron answered. He was in the doorway now. "You rolled over on one of your own because you were scared of getting in trouble."

"He's not one of my own. I hate him. If he gets in trouble that's his problem, not mine."

Aaron stepped into the kitchen but looked back to say, "Your problem is you were born without guts."

"Who's Spencer Randle?" Evan asked.

"Nobody."

"What did you do to him?"

"Nothing. I don't want to talk about it."

Evan poked me with the lacrosse stick. "Tell me. Is he a friend of yours?"

"Let's see," I said. "In kindergarten he pushed me into the mud. In second grade he stole my cupcake and ate it in front of me. In fourth grade he locked me in the janitor's closet during the school ice cream party. Last year he dunked my clothes in the toilet during gym class. And earlier this week he stole my lunch money. So no, he's not really a friend. Oh, and now, he wants to smash my face in because I told the principal he was going to Pilchuck Market for a corn dog."

Evan chewed on her thumbnail. "So don't let him," she said casually.

"You don't understand," I said, closing *Frankenstein*. "Spencer Randle is a monster. If he really does

43

know it was me who told on him, he's going to use my face as his own personal punching bag."

"Then you're a chicken," Evan said.

"Thanks," I said. "I prefer to think of it as sensible."

"So you're just going to hide from him for the rest of your life?"

"You have a better idea?"

"Yeah," said Evan. "Turn the tables. You find him. Tell him it was you and that you'll do it again if you have to."

"Are you nuts? He'll squash me."

"From what you're saying, it sounds like he was going to do that anyway. If you confront him, at least you get it over with." Evan peeled herself up from the back of the chair, stretching out her arms and yawning. "Or maybe you'll pop him one and earn a little respect for once."

I watched the mosquitoes swarm around the porch light while Evan's last words swarmed in my head. Did she mean that I needed to earn a little respect from Spencer Randle, or from her? Because I didn't really care what Spencer thought about me, but I sure cared what Evan thought.

A few minutes later, Mom poked her head outside. "Oh, hi, Evan," she said. "How are you?"

"I'm good, Mrs. Parker," Evan replied, craning her neck to look Mom in the eye.

"Wyatt, it's time to come inside," Mom said.

"I should go anyway," Evan said with a wave. "In a while, crocodile."

"On your pillow, armadillo," I replied.

Evan laughed as she disappeared around the fence. I went inside smiling. *Let's see Brian Braun make Evan laugh like that,* I thought.

CHAPTER SIX

After the PA incident, Mr. Groton suspended Spencer
for the rest of that week and the whole next week, so
the hallways of Pilchuck Middle School were safe for
seven whole school days. I knew it was only tempo-
rary, but I tried to enjoy the peace. I even ate lunch
outside again. I tried to convince Francis to come
too, but he went back to Mr. Leland's room.

McKlusky and Raj were on the grass, throwing
the football. "You want to play?" McKlusky asked,
tossing the ball to me.

"Sure," I said, catching the pass.

We passed the ball around until the bell rang. Raj
showed me how to grip with my hand farther back

on the ball. Pretty soon, I was throwing faster and straighter and catching almost everything. I wished Evan could see me.

Catching a football was great, but it was nothing compared to what happened in my baseball game on Saturday. Even though it was only a rec league game, I would never forget the way it ended. And Evan was there to see it all.

It was the final inning of our last game of the season and we were down a run. I was on second base, Julian was on third, Fish was at the plate. If I made it home, we'd win, and we'd go down to Corner Pizza to celebrate. If I didn't score, we'd end the season without a win, and we'd probably go down in history as the worst rec league baseball team in the world. I was so focused on not blowing the game, I wasn't even thinking about Spencer Randle.

I was running the instant Fish hit the ball, leaving second base behind in a cloud of dust. Ahead of me, Julian was cruising for home. He was the tying run. That meant it was up to me to win the game. I had to cross the plate before the right fielder got the ball to the catcher. Pumping my arms, I breathed deep, forcing my legs to go faster than they had ever gone. I must have been doing fifty miles an hour by the time I got to third base.

Coach Darby stood in front of the dugout, waving

me around the bag. "Go, Wyatt, go!" he yelled. His face was red and pages flew off his clipboard as he swung it wildly.

I charged down the third-base line.

The rest of the guys were jumping up and down. McKlusky clutched his hat. Luther, Shane, and Caleb cheered. Kenny fell to his knees and beat the ground with his hands. Roy, who had bunted me over to second, pointed to the ground with a bat.

I saw the catcher squatting next to the plate. He stuck his right arm straight up into the sky, reaching for the ball. I decided he wasn't a person, just a thing in my way.

I had time for one more breath before I slid.

I took a big gulp of air, then hit the dirt. Tucking my right leg under my body, I stuck my left foot out and skidded toward the plate.

The umpire yanked his mask off.

The first part of me to hit the catcher was my right knee, which hurt because I was going fast and he was wearing plastic armor on his legs. Then he fell on me. That hurt even more because I was small and he was big. He tagged me with the ball in his glove.

But my left leg was already on the plate.

The umpire aimed a finger at my leg before hollering *"Safe!"* so loud his call echoed off the wall of the grandstand.

Hands reached down and pulled me up.

"You did it, Wyatt!" someone yelled. "You won the game!"

I was so happy. I had never done anything like that in my life. I had never won the game. But I'd done it now. I'd knocked that catcher over and scored the winning run in the last inning of our last game of the season. All ninety-eight pounds of me had taken down the thing in my way. I wondered what else I could knock down.

Could I knock down Spencer Randle?

My whole team mobbed me. They pounded on my helmet and slapped me on the back. I smiled the whole time, even though being hit on the head by eight guys who were all bigger than me was kind of painful.

When the celebration finally ended, I saw Mom and Dad clapping in the bleachers, but it was Evan I wanted to see the most. I broke away from the pack and found her hanging out with a group of her friends from her school, Parkside.

After slipping away from them, she stuck out her fist. "That was so cool," she said.

It might have been my imagination, but I thought Evan was looking at me the same way she had looked at Brian Braun right before we saw *Swing and a Miss*.

I bumped my fist into hers. "Thanks. I'm not even hurt."

Evan pointed to my leg. "You might feel it later. Sometimes after a game I'm so amped up I don't realize something hurts until the next day, and then it's like, oh man, ouch, when did I do that? But I'm sure you'll be fine."

McKlusky ran over and grabbed my arm. "Pizza," he said. "Now."

Evan pointed at her friends, who were talking to Julian, Shane, and Luther, who also went to Parkside. "I gotta go too," she said. "I'll see you soon."

I watched Evan run back to the Parkside girls. I was so happy it didn't even bother me when I saw her chatting with Julian. After all, he hadn't scored the winning run. I had.

Pizza never tasted so good. "Hey, Wyatt," said Caleb when we were eating. "You really dumped that catcher on his butt."

"Yeah," McKlusky added. "You looked like a running back."

That was when Julian walked by our table. "Did I hear you right?" he asked, stopping suddenly. "Did I just hear someone say Wyatt could be a running back?"

So much for being the hero, I thought, feeling half as big as I had a minute ago.

"What's so crazy about Wyatt being a running back?" Caleb asked.

Julian pointed at me. "You're talking about this Wyatt, right? He wouldn't gain a single yard."

I just looked straight ahead, hoping they'd walk away. Luckily, Julian went over to the video games, leaving me with McKlusky and Caleb.

"How come you let him talk to you like that?" Caleb asked.

"What am I supposed to do? He's bigger than me."

"It's not always about who's bigger," Caleb replied.

Roy sat down across from me. "Caleb's right," he said. "That catcher was bigger than you. And you flattened him like a pancake." He pushed up his sleeves and surveyed the pizza. "If you ran at them like that, they'd probably be afraid of you."

"Yeah, right," I said, picking up a breadstick instead.

"I'm serious," Roy replied. "You were like a wild animal out there. *I'm* a little afraid of you."

"Me too," said McKlusky, nodding with his mouth full. "You should play football in the park with us sometime. It's just for fun."

"Listen to him," Roy said. "Nobody messes with football players. And then there's the girls."

"Yeah," said Caleb. "And this summer there's a flag football league at the rec center."

"I don't know," I told them. "I might be going to golf camp."

"Golf camp?" Roy asked in disbelief. He grabbed his sides and pretended to laugh. "You're kidding, right?"

"It wasn't my idea," I said, wishing I hadn't mentioned it.

"Here's some free advice," said Roy, wiping his face. "If anyone ever asks you if you're going to golf camp, do yourself a favor and lie."

"What's so bad about golf camp?" I asked.

"Nothing," said Caleb. "If you're a hundred."

"Stick with football," said Roy, grabbing the last slice of pizza. "Or baseball. Anything but golf."

When the pizza was all gone, it was time to leave. McKlusky and I found our bags and headed for the door. "Like I said, a bunch of us play football in the park on weekends, usually around noon. It's just two-hand touch. No tackling."

"I'll see if I can make it," I said as McKlusky and I headed off in opposite directions. There was no doubt in my mind, I wanted to play football with McKlusky and the other guys. The question was whether Mom would let me. And that was something I didn't think McKlusky really needed to know.

Who cared what Mom thought, anyway? I could handle a game of football. Maybe I'd even plow over someone like I'd plowed over that catcher. Replaying the collision in my mind, I remembered how my teammates had slapped me on the back. And I could still hear Caleb telling me I should play football. I knew for sure there was no way I would ever feel that way playing golf.

By the time I got to my house, I was six inches taller than I had been when I'd left. And then I did something really, really dumb.

CHAPTER SEVEN

When I got home, I could hear Mom and Dad talking in the kitchen about their work schedules. There was no sign of Aaron or Kate. Quietly, I found the school directory we kept by the telephone in the living room.

I looked up Randle and found the number. Then I dialed. My heart was pounding, but I willed myself not to hang up. I was starting a new life. I wasn't going to be afraid anymore. I was going to earn a little respect.

Besides, what did I have to lose? Spencer already knew it was me. Or at least that was what I thought.

"Who's this?" Spencer asked when he came to the phone.

"This is Wyatt Parker," I said clearly. "The guy who told on you."

"That was *you*?" he asked. "You got me suspended for more than a week. Groton said he would have suspended me for the rest of the year but he wants me to come back for the last week so I can end on a positive note. Can you believe that garbage?"

My mouth dried up like the desert. "You s-s-said you knew who it was," I stammered.

"I thought it was that punk Morelli," Spencer said. "He's got the biggest mouth in school. I was looking forward to shutting it for him. But I guess I'll have to teach you a lesson instead."

This was not going the way I had thought it would. I tried to get back some of the courage I had felt earlier. I remembered what Evan had said about turning the tables on Spencer. "Or maybe I'll teach you a lesson," I said, my voice quavering.

"Are you crazy?" Spencer asked. "You're threatening me? Nobody threatens me."

"That wasn't a threat. That was a promise. I didn't threaten you."

"I promise you," Spencer growled, "I am going to make you regret picking up the phone."

"Well, I'm going to make you regret answering it."

"You just don't know when to stop talking, do you?" Spencer asked.

"Apparently not."

"Good. When I get back to school, we can talk all day long, if you know what I mean."

The line went dead.

• • •

I didn't feel like talking during dinner. Luckily Dad was busy with Aaron. "Have you found anything to do this summer?" he asked. "If the answer is no, you're going to be stuffing envelopes at my office. All day, all week, all summer."

"I'm volunteering in the park," Aaron replied.

That surprised me. I couldn't picture Aaron volunteering. Unless it was volunteering to steal golf carts and roll them into sand traps, which is what he did last summer.

Dad was surprised too. "Really?" he asked. "Volunteering how?"

"Um, just cleaning up trash and clearing trails."

"Did you hear about this at school?" asked Mom.

"Yup, at school." Aaron kept his eyes on his plate. "Oh, I need one of those orange vests. For safety."

"Well, good for you, Aaron," said Dad, nodding proudly. "I'm glad you found something productive to do."

They seemed so happy that I decided to speak up after all. "Can I play flag football?"

Dad leaned back in his chair. "What was that?" he asked.

"Some friends of mine are playing flag football this summer. Can I play too?"

"You're going to golf camp," Dad replied.

"With me," Kate reminded everyone. "And my new clubs."

"Only if you get a B on that math test," Mom reminded her.

I kept working on Dad, hoping for a break. "Golf camp isn't all summer."

"When does football start?"

"I don't know," I admitted. "I just heard about it today."

Dad looked skeptical. "This doesn't sound very well thought out."

"Or safe," Mom added.

"There's no tackling or anything," I explained.

"I think the answer is no," Mom replied. "After golf camp, if you still want to try another sport, we can find something for you. Maybe tennis. Or swimming."

I remembered Roy telling me that nobody messed with football players. I doubted anyone ever said nobody messes with tennis players.

● ● ●

After dinner I went to the back porch to read, but the armchair was occupied. Aaron was picking pieces of lint out of the fabric of the cushion and tossing them absentmindedly into the darkness.

"What are you doing here?" I asked. "Shouldn't you be on the phone with your girlfriend?"

"I don't have a girlfriend," Aaron mumbled.

"What?" I said, taking a seat on the porch swing where Evan usually sat.

"I. Don't. Have. A. Girlfriend," he said again. "She dumped me."

"Didn't you take her to River Tunes?"

"It has nothing to do with River Tunes," Aaron snapped. "She dumped me because she doesn't appreciate me." He pounded on one of the arms of the chair. "Man! I can't wait for summer. I am going to break someone's bones."

"Picking up trash?" I asked.

"I'm not picking up any trash."

"What do you mean? What about your volunteer job at the park?"

"Are you nuts?" Aaron said. "I'm not volunteering in the park. I'm playing football."

Sensing something big, I sat up straight. "You are? Where?"

"None of your business."

"Please tell me."

"No, and don't ask me again. And don't even think about telling Mom and Dad what I told you."

"Is it flag football? Because a bunch of my friends are—"

"It's not flag football. Give me a break."

Aaron was right, that was a dumb question. But the more he refused to tell me where he was playing football, the more I had to know the truth. "Is it at the high school?"

"I told you not to ask me again," Aaron said, getting out of the armchair. "I'm going inside." He kicked a bucket of lawn darts that had been sitting upright on the porch. Darts and hoops spilled everywhere. "Don't follow me."

With frogs croaking in the background, I pushed myself back and forth on the swing and thought more about my conversation with Aaron. It was easy to believe he would make up a story about volunteering in the park to get Mom and Dad off his back. But I couldn't figure out the football part. Mom and Dad already let him play football. Why would he need to lie to them about playing this summer? Did he think Mom and Dad wouldn't believe he'd be able to do both? Suddenly, it was all I could think about.

I tried to distract myself by reading more of *Frankenstein*. When that didn't work, I went to my computer and searched for *football leagues in Pilchuck* and got about a ton of links to stories about Pilchuck High School. So I typed in *football leagues in Pilchuck summer,* but I didn't find anything except the flag football league at the rec center.

I fell asleep that night wondering what Aaron was up to and how I could get in on it, because whatever it was sounded like a lot more fun than golf camp.

CHAPTER EIGHT

"Maybe he got recruited for a secret team that plays football during the day and fights crime at night," Evan guessed on Tuesday evening.

She was in her usual spot on the porch and I was a few feet away in the armchair. "I don't think so," I said. "Aaron causes crime. He doesn't fight it."

"Are we even sure it's football? He might be doing something he's too embarrassed to tell anyone about, like ice-skating or chess."

"Trust me, Aaron only knows two things, football and . . . actually, he only knows one thing." I tilted my neck back and stared up at the sky. "Argh, I have to know what it is!"

"Why do you care so much?" Evan asked.

"I care because . . . why should Aaron get to play football this summer while I have to play golf? It's not fair."

Evan narrowed her eyes and tilted her head to the side. "Wait, you want to play football?" She said it like she hadn't heard me right.

"Don't act so surprised," I said. "I've played football before."

"Tell me one time you played football."

"Okay, maybe I can't think of a time right now, but that doesn't mean I'm never allowed to play. Isn't there a first time for everything?"

"You really want to play football?" Evan said again, the disbelief in her voice fading. "Like with pads and helmets?"

"I haven't thought that much about it," I said. "I just want to try it."

Evan's eyes sparkled. "Go, Wyatt! That's so cool. You should definitely try it. I saw the sign-up sheet for the flag football league at the rec center. Did you ask your parents yet?"

"They're thinking it over," I explained, reluctant to admit they had already said no. Not when I had finally found someone who was on my side. "My mom is afraid I might get hurt. I mean, I'm not the biggest guy in the world."

"So what? There was this girl on my lacrosse team last year who was short, but she was a total star because nobody could check her."

"Why not?"

"She was too quick."

"You really think I could play football?"

"Yes, I do," Evan said. "I bet you could even be on the freshman team next year."

"No way."

"Way. All you need is practice." Evan poked me in the ribs. "And a few meals. Oh, and you have to let me watch a game." She shook her head. "I never thought I would get to see Wyatt Parker playing football," she added, hopping off the swing. "Gotta run."

I slapped her hand as she passed by. "Toodle-oo, kangaroo."

"Keep it real, harbor seal."

Not long after Evan left, the screen door flew open and Aaron appeared on the porch. "Are you any good at geometry?" he asked.

"Geometry?"

"Yeah, geometry. You know, like shapes. I have to do all these calculations and I think my teacher might have explained it all on a day I was out. So, can you help me?"

"Fine," I said. I stood halfway up, then sat back

down. "Hold on. If you want my help, you need to tell me where you're playing football this summer."

Aaron's face went tense. He closed the door behind him and made a slashing motion across his throat. "What are you doing?" he hissed. "I told you not to say anything about that."

"Do you want my help or not?"

Aaron rolled his eyes upward and bit down on his lip. "Okay," he said. "I'll tell you . . ."

I pumped my fist. "Yes!"

". . . after you help me."

"Deal," I said, jumping to my feet.

It took me about an hour to teach Aaron how to calculate the angle of a triangle using the lengths of the sides. I could have taught him to do it the other way around too, but I was afraid his brain would overheat.

"Thanks," he said, closing his book. "You really saved me."

"Yeah, yeah. Talk to me about football."

Aaron was about to answer when there was a knock on the door. "What?" he barked.

"Mom wants you to take out the garbage," said Kate, sticking her head into Aaron's room.

"Got it."

Kate didn't move.

"Why are you still here?" Aaron asked.

A smile crept across Kate's face. "What were you guys talking about? Will you tell me?"

"It was nothing," I said. "I was just helping him with his math."

Kate didn't buy it. "I can keep a secret," she promised. "Please tell me."

"Man!" Aaron cried. "Why does everyone in this house have to know everything?"

Kate stepped farther into the room. "So there *is* a secret. I knew it! Are you in trouble? Did you get a new girlfriend? Is Sara mad?"

"Scram," said Aaron. "Now." He looked over at me. "Both of you."

"Hey! We had a deal."

Aaron pushed me and Kate out of his room and shut the door. "Deal's off," he said from the other side of the wall.

"I'm not giving up!" I yelled back. "I will learn the truth!"

"The truth about what?" Kate asked.

"The truth about nothing," I said.

"If it's nothing, why can't you tell me?"

"Because I don't even know it," I shot back, leaving her alone in the hallway.

● ● ●

The next day at school, Francis caught up with me at my locker. "What are you doing Saturday?" he asked.

"Not sure," I said with my back turned. "Why?"

"The amateur golf championship is about an hour north of here. I know they're not pros, but some of them will be soon. We can say we saw them before they were famous."

After zipping up my backpack, I faced Francis. He looked like a dog that wanted me to throw a ball. I wished he would go with his dad without asking me. "You want to just go to the golf course and watch other people play?"

"Yeah," said Francis. "We'll follow the players along the course. Sometimes they sign autographs. There's food too. It's a lot of fun."

Why couldn't I just tell Francis the whole truth right then? That I didn't think the golf tournament sounded fun. That I didn't want to go to golf camp or play in the father-son tournament. That I didn't even like golf. It would have been the right thing to do, but I was too afraid of hurting his feelings, so I lied.

"Sure," I said. "That sounds like fun."

CHAPTER NINE

On Saturday morning I got on my bike to ride to Boardman Park. McKlusky had invited me on Friday night to play football with him and some of the other guys from school. I told him yes right away, and I was glad I did. It was the first Saturday in June, the sun was out, and I was going to do what I wanted to do.

Mom found me in the driveway. She was just coming home from an overnight shift at the hospital. Aaron was lifting weights in the garage.

"Where are you going?" she asked me.

"To meet some friends."

"How nice," Mom said. "I'm going shopping, but I'll be home by two. Call if you need anything."

Aaron sat up on the bench. "That's it?" he asked. "You're not even going to ask him what he's doing? You don't let me go anywhere without asking me what I'm doing."

"We trust Wyatt," said Mom.

"Real nice," Aaron grumbled, lying back down.

Sometimes it's easier being the good one, I thought as I rode away from the house.

As the sun burned through the late-morning clouds, I coasted down the windy road that twisted and turned under the shade of giant elm trees. I pedaled past the grandstand where the Pilchuck All-Stars were warming up for a baseball game, rode over the footbridge that crossed the stream, and followed the path toward the back of the park. That was when I saw McKlusky and Caleb.

They were standing with two small groups on a grassy field. Caleb was holding a football.

"Hey, Wyatt!" McKlusky called with a wave as he came running over. "You made it! So, you want in?"

I slid off my bike seat and straddled the crossbar with my feet on the ground. "Is there room?" I asked, watching Raj and Khalil placing cones at either end of the field.

McKlusky nodded. "We've got nine. If you play with us, we'll have even teams. We were going to play with a permanent quarterback, but it's more fun the real way." McKlusky held up two hands. "I mean, two-hand-touch real. Not tackle real.

"I know it's kind of lame," McKlusky said as we hustled over to the other guys. "But if we play tackle, then the team that has Khalil just hands it off to him every time because nobody can bring him down."

I ended up on a team with Caleb, Khalil, Roy, and Kenny. Kenny explained the rules while Roy and Fish argued over who was going to get the ball first. "It's pretty simple," said Kenny, brushing back the mop of hair hanging over his eyes. He was wearing cargo shorts and sneakers with no socks. "We play two-hand touch, two completions, ten Mississippi, no tackling."

I wasn't sure what all that meant, but I pretended I did by nodding. "What position should I play?" I asked Caleb when we huddled up for the first time.

"We kind of rotate," Caleb explained. "I'm going to start at quarterback. You're fast, so why don't you go deep? Morelli, you run a fifteen-step post route with a buttonhook."

"Make it twenty steps," said Roy. "I'm feelin' it."

I made a note to watch Roy run so I'd know what a post route with a buttonhook was.

"What about me?" Kenny asked.

"You line up on the right. But go in motion left after Khalil snaps the ball. I'll fake the hand-off."

"I guess that means I'm fake running," said Kenny, shaking his head.

"And I'm fake blocking," Khalil added.

Caleb held out his hand. "On two," he whispered to Khalil.

We put our hands on Caleb's and broke the huddle. He lined up behind Khalil, who bent over with the ball between his hands. Roy lined up to his right with Kenny a little farther over. I wasn't sure where to go, so I stood on Caleb's left.

Raj lined up across from me. He was about my size, so it made sense that he was guarding me. "Don't plan on getting open," he said with a smile.

I was glad Raj was defending me. I was pretty sure he wouldn't make fun of me if I didn't know what to do. "Hey," I asked him as Khalil got ready to snap the ball. "How far is deep?"

"What?"

"Caleb told me to go deep. How far is deep?"

"See that tree behind me with the bike leaning against it?"

"Yeah," I said, spotting a maple tree about a hundred feet away.

"Run past that and you'll be deep." Raj looked over at Caleb. "But in the future, don't tell the defense where the quarterback told you to run."

A second later, the play began. Caleb stood right

behind Khalil. "Green thirty-six!" he barked. "Green thirty-six! On two. Hut-hut . . . hike!" He took the ball from Khalil, then dropped back five steps as Kenny ran behind him.

"One Mississippi," I heard McKlusky say.

I didn't see what happened next, though, because I was running downfield as fast as I could with Raj right beside me. I kept my head down for speed and didn't look back until I'd passed the maple tree. When I was sure I was deep, I came to a stop and got ready to catch the ball if Caleb threw it to me. Except by then, Roy had the football and was running full speed on the other side of the field. Everyone, including Raj, was chasing him. Before I figured out what I was supposed to do, Roy was in the end zone, where he spiked the ball and held out his arms in triumph.

"Seven–nothing, losers!" he shouted.

Then it was our turn on defense. While the other team huddled, Roy came up to me. "You're going to rush the QB," he said.

"Um, okay."

"You have no idea what that means, do you?" he asked.

I didn't answer.

Roy pointed to Fish, who was playing quarterback for the other team. "As soon as Fish gets the football

71

in his hands, count out loud to ten like this: one Mississippi, two Mississippi, three Mississippi. When you get to ten Mississippi, blitz him."

"Blitz him?"

"Yeah, blitz him," Roy said again. "Run after him as fast as you can and try to tag him. Got it?"

"Got it," I said, excited to finally have something to do. I didn't want to mess it up.

"Oh, one more thing," said Roy. "Fish can't cross the line of scrimmage until you get to ten."

"That's the imaginary line between us and them when the play starts," Roy whispered.

The play started. McKlusky snapped the ball to Fish and I started counting. "One Mississippi, two Mississippi, three Mississippi." At first Fish stood in one place with the ball in his right hand. He looked downfield for a receiver.

"Seven Mississippi," I called.

"Someone get open!" Fish yelled, hopping up and down.

"Eight Mississippi, nine Mississippi . . ."

Then, before I got to ten Mississippi, Fish crossed the line of scrimmage and began running full speed downfield, and didn't stop until he was in the end zone with Roy running behind him.

"Eat it!" he shouted at Roy.

"You eat it," Roy shot back, his hands on his knees.

"He crossed the line before I got to ten," I told Roy.

"He what?" Roy asked, glaring at Fish. "I knew it." He ran back to the end zone. "Gimme the ball, cheater," he said to Fish.

"Who cheated?" Fish asked. "I didn't cheat."

"You crossed the line of scrimmage early."

"Please, even if I did, you were fifty yards away."

"Wyatt saw it," Roy said. "And he wouldn't lie."

"Why not?" Fish asked.

"He barely knows the rules. How could he lie about them?"

"I heard him say ten," Fish insisted.

"Liar."

"I wasn't over the line," Fish said. "I was like this." He put himself into a running pose with his back foot up and his front foot planted. "I didn't go forward until he said ten."

Caleb jumped in next. "Now I know you're lying," he told Fish. "Wyatt never *said* ten."

"That's not our fault," Raj added.

Roy, Julian, Caleb, Fish, and Raj kept arguing for a long time. I was beginning to wonder if the game would ever start again. It didn't seem like anyone was going to give in. Finally, Kenny said, "Just do it over." They all agreed.

This time I counted my Mississippis loudly enough that everyone could hear me. When I got to four,

Fish threw a short pass to Raj, but Raj dropped the ball. It rolled toward me.

I had seen this happen in the games I watched with Aaron and Dad. Whenever the ball fell on the ground like that, one of the players picked it up and ran the other way. Without wasting a second, I grabbed the ball, tucked it under my arm, and ran as fast as I could for the end zone. I was sure Raj would be hot on my heels to tag me. But he never caught me. I was in the end zone! Touchdown!

I spun around. "Eat it!" I shouted, just like Roy had.

They were all standing back at the spot where Raj had dropped the ball. Nobody had run after me.

"Dude," said Khalil. "What are you doing? That was an incomplete pass. You can't score off an incomplete pass."

"Oh," I said, joining my team in the huddle. "I didn't know."

"Well, now you do," Roy said. "Can we get ready for the next play? If we stop them here, we'll get the ball back, and we'll have a chance to win." Roy lifted his head and looked over at the other team. "Hey, next score wins!"

"Cool," Fish shouted back.

The play began when Raj snapped the ball. I followed him as he ran across the middle of the field.

Fish fired a pass to Raj and he caught it without slowing down. Raj took two steps and turned to run downfield. That was when he lost his grip on the ball. It fell to the ground.

Incomplete pass! We still had a chance to win.

I jogged toward Roy and Caleb, who were running toward me.

"Get the ball!" Roy shouted.

I wasn't sure what the big deal was. Why did he want me to pick up the ball so quickly? It was our turn no matter what.

"Fumble!" Caleb yelled.

I looked back at the ball in time to see Fish snatch it. He cruised to the end zone, high-stepping all the way.

"Oh yeah, that's right, that happened, oh yeah, that's right, that happened," he chanted, dancing around in a circle and holding the ball with his arms outstretched. Soon the whole team was doing it too. "Oh yeah, that's right, that happened."

"I want to puke," Roy grumbled. "Why didn't you pick it up?" he asked me.

"It was an incomplete pass," I said.

Caleb shook his head. "It's not an incomplete pass if he catches the ball, runs with it, and then drops it. Then it's a fumble."

"Oh," I said. "I guess I didn't know that."

"I guess not," said Roy sarcastically. He shook his head slowly. "Maybe football isn't your sport after all."

Walking back to my bike, I looked down at the grass and dirt stains on my hands, knees, and clothes. I hadn't taken a beating, but I had played football, and nobody could take that away from me. And maybe I hadn't played well, but I remembered how it felt to be the hero in my baseball game after failing so many times before that. If I could get better at baseball, I was sure I could get better at football too. I set out with plenty of time to get home, washed up, and changed before Mom saw me.

• • •

When I got back to the house, Kate was in the backyard unrolling Dad's putting green. It was a long, narrow rug with a hole at one end and a spot to putt from on the other end. A putter lay in the grass next to a bucket of golf balls.

"Guess what?" she said. "I know the big secret. Aaron has a new girlfriend, just like I said. Her name is Olivia."

"That's not the big secret," I said, rushing to the back door.

"Then what is?" Kate asked, following me into the house.

I responded without turning around. "I don't know, but I know that's not it."

Kate's reply froze me in my tracks. "Francis called here like three times. Mom talked to his mom. I think you're in trouble."

I had forgotten all about the golf tournament Francis had invited me to! I had a feeling things were about to get complicated.

When I walked through the back door, Mom was waiting. "Wyatt, where were you? And why are you so dirty? What were you doing?"

"I was with my friends," I said.

"What friends?" she asked, eyeing my dirt-caked legs and shorts.

I stood behind a chair. "Just some guys from school. You don't know them."

"What were you doing?"

I hesitated before answering. I wasn't sure if I should tell Mom the truth. Lately, telling the truth had not worked out so well for me. But how mad could Mom get about one football game? "We were playing football."

"Football?" Mom said. "I thought we already talked about this. No football."

"It was just two-hand—"

"We'll talk about that later," Mom interrupted. "Why didn't you go to the tournament with Francis today? He said you made plans."

"I know. I forgot."

"Wyatt, when someone invites you to do something and you accept the invitation, you cannot just forget. What you did was incredibly rude."

"I'm sorry," I said.

"I'm not the one you need to apologize to," Mom answered. "Now go upstairs. You can call Francis after dinner."

"I'll see him Monday."

Mom stood in the doorway. "Not Monday," she said. "I want you to call Francis tonight."

I wished I could run right through Mom and keep going. I was so sick of doing whatever anybody told me to do when other people just did whatever they wanted. In fact, this made me want to play football even more. "Fine," I said, gritting my teeth. "I'll call him later and say I'm sorry."

"And say it like you mean it, Wyatt."

I wanted to kick a hole in the wall. It wasn't enough to tell me what to say, Mom also had to tell me how to say it. Still, I couldn't bring myself to tell her how I felt, so instead I took a deep breath. "Okay. I'll say it like I mean it," I promised, ducking under her arm on my way out of the kitchen.

Upstairs, Aaron was studying himself in the mirror and whistling to music. "Come in here," he said as I passed by the bathroom.

"What?"

"Did you play football after Mom specifically told you not to?" Aaron asked without taking his eyes off himself.

"Yes," I admitted. "Why?"

"Would you do it again? I'm asking you man to man, so tell the truth."

I got the feeling he was being serious. "Yeah, I would do it again," I said. "It's worth it, even if I get in trouble."

"In that case," said Aaron, slapping aftershave on his face, "maybe you're ready after all."

I winced as the odor hit me. "Ready for what?"

Aaron kicked the bathroom door shut. "To learn about the League of Pain," he said.

CHAPTER TEN

My mind was racing one hundred miles an hour. Did I hear Aaron right? Did he say the League of Pain? What kind of football league was that?

Aaron lowered the lid over the toilet seat and directed me to sit down. "First, I'm going to give you a little advice," he began. "Never, ever tell Mom you're playing football. That was a mistake you cannot repeat."

"Okay, don't tell Mom about football. Got it. What is the League of Pain?"

"It's our own league," Aaron explained. "We play in the park and we make our own rules. And nobody knows about it except the people who play in it."

"Who plays in it?" I asked.

"Some people you know and some people you don't know," Aaron answered.

"Can I play?"

"You can watch. That's all I can promise."

"When?"

"Our first game is at noon on the first Monday of summer vacation."

"That's the first day of golf camp," I said.

Aaron shrugged. "That's your problem."

That was a problem, but I had already made up my mind that I was not going to golf camp. *I* was going to choose what I did this summer, not Mom or Dad.

"Remember," Aaron added. "Never, ever tell Mom you were playing football."

"You really think I should lie?"

"It's your life, not hers," Aaron said. "If you want to live it your way, sometimes you're going to have to tell her what she wants to hear and keep the rest to yourself."

"Why did you change your mind?" I asked. "Why are you telling me all this now?"

"It's like this," Aaron replied. "Things are going pretty good in my life. If you show up at school in the fall acting like the helpless dweeb you are now, it could be bad for business—for me. So I figure if you see a little combat over the summer, you might grow a spine and not totally destroy the Parker name. That's the idea, anyway."

"I'm not a dweeb," I said. "I played football today, remember?"

Aaron opened the bathroom door. "Two-hand-touch football, and yes, you are," he said, showing me out. "But don't feel bad. This is just me being honest, brother to brother. Now go. I have a date tonight."

Out in the hallway, Mom was pestering Kate about her math homework. "Is it done?" she asked.

"No," Kate admitted. "It's too hard."

"I don't think you tried," Mom responded.

"Can Wyatt help me?"

Mom shook her head. "No, you need to do it," she said, looking at both of us.

"He helped Aaron with his homework."

"My answer is no, Kate," Mom said, shooing Kate to her room. "Now get to it. Your test is in less than a week."

"I know that," Kate said. "And by the way, it's take-home, so stop stressing."

"Get to work," Mom said again.

Back in my room, I picked up the football and ran around in short spurts, pretending to dodge invisible tacklers on my way to the end zone. In just over a week, I'd be doing it for real in an actual football game. I was so happy about the idea of playing I didn't even care that I'd be in something called the League of Pain. I already felt like Brian Braun.

A knock on the door interrupted my celebration. "Is everything okay?" Mom asked.

"Yep," I said. "Everything's fine. I'm just doing my homework for, um, gym class."

"Did you call Francis?"

"Not yet."

"Call him now, Wyatt."

"Fine."

I picked up the phone, then decided it would be easier to send Francis a text. *Sorry about today. Something came up. Later.* I set the phone down and spent the next twenty minutes trying to spin the football on my finger.

CHAPTER ELEVEN

"Can you believe it's almost summer?" Evan asked, swatting at a mosquito later that night. "I'm so ready for school to be over."

"I don't know," I said. "I kind of like school."

"You're such a nerd." Evan slugged me gently on the shoulder to let me know she was kidding.

"Whatever, tomboy."

Evan socked me again. This time, it wasn't gentle. "Don't call me that, Wyatt. I told you I hate that."

I rubbed my shoulder. "Well, maybe I hate being called a nerd."

We were quiet for a few minutes. It wasn't a good

silence, like when one of us looked for the shooting stars while the other person read, or when we were sitting in a theater waiting for a movie to begin.

Evan was the first one to speak. "Sorry I punched you."

"That's okay," I said. "It didn't hurt."

"Liar."

"Hey, I could have punched you back."

Evan batted her eyes. "You'd never hit a lady, Wyatt. That's what I like about you."

"Call me a nerd one more time and see what happens."

Evan laughed. Suddenly, she sat straight up in the lawn chair. "Oh, I totally forgot to tell you. I got a job at the pool this summer. Well, not a job exactly. But I'm going to be a junior swim instructor. You know, like helping the real instructors teach swim lessons." Evan pretended to do the crawl stroke. "I'm so excited! I get a free pass to the pool *all summer,* and when I'm sixteen it's almost automatic that I'll get to be a lifeguard."

Evan leaped up and started dancing around the porch. "Go, Evan. Go, Evan. Go, Evan." Then she froze. "And guess who else works at the pool? Ooh la la, Brian Braun. He was there when I turned in my application and he was like, are you working here this summer, and I think I said, um, yes, but I might not have said anything, I don't know, and he said, cool, I'll show you around."

"Around where?" I asked, even though I didn't care.

"The pool, I guess. But isn't that great? Now I'll have something to talk to him about next year. You should meet him, Wyatt. You'd totally like him. He's a really nice guy."

"Woo-hoo."

"Wyatt, this is a really big deal. It's like a job." Evan sat back on the porch swing. "I didn't tell you the other best part. I met a bunch of the other people who are going to work at the pool and they invited me to watch the fireworks on the hill. You should come."

I was pretty sure who else was in that group, which meant I was out. The last thing I wanted to do was hike up some hill so I could watch fireworks with Evan and Brian Braun, even though I thought he was pretty much the coolest guy in Pilchuck.

"I don't know if I can," I told Evan. "I might be folding American flags at the retirement home."

"Um, okay," she answered. "Well, when you get done with that, you should come find us."

I told Evan I would think about it, but I had already made up my mind. Evan and I had never hung out in groups, and I didn't want to hang out with Evan in a group now. I wanted to hang out with Evan by myself.

I went to my room and found Kate in my beanbag chair, reading a book. I pointed to the door. "Good night."

"Why don't you want to watch the fireworks with Evan?" she asked.

"Were you listening?"

"The window was open. Why don't you want to watch the fireworks with Evan?"

"Who said I didn't?"

"You told her you had to think about it. That's the same thing. Why don't you want to watch the fireworks with Evan?"

I sat on my bed. "Because she's going to be with a bunch of people I don't know and there's nothing fun about that."

"But she invited you."

"I don't want to go," I said.

"Why don't you just admit you like her?" Kate asked me.

I looked at Kate. "Like her?"

"*Like her* like her," she said.

"I don't want to talk about this with you."

Kate didn't care. "You should tell her. She might like you too."

"We're just friends. That's all. She likes Brian Brian. I mean Braun."

"Who's Brian Braun?"

"He's a lifeguard. At the pool. Where Evan is working this summer. He has more muscles than Batman. You see what I'm saying?"

"You should watch the fireworks with her. She might get scared and grab your hand."

"Then what?"

Kate looked at me like I was crazy. "You don't know?" she asked.

I shrugged. "Sorry."

"Hold it back, dummy." She shook her head as she walked out of the room. "Hopeless," I heard her say as she padded down the hallway.

Suddenly, I couldn't get the thought of holding Evan's hand out of my mind. Could that really happen watching fireworks? How would I know when to let go? What if I never let go? Would we just hold hands all the way through high school? We'd have to take all the same classes and sit next to each other. That didn't sound too bad.

The next time I saw Evan I was going to tell her I'd changed my mind about watching the fireworks. Which meant Brian Braun wouldn't be the only football player on the hill that night.

CHAPTER TWELVE

I was looking forward to the fireworks, but I'd have to wait. The Fourth of July was still a month away. I needed to make it through another week and a half of school before I could even think about summer. On Monday I was bending down to find my math book when I heard a familiar voice.

"Miss me?"

I looked up to see Spencer Randle, and gulped. Had it been a week already?

"Not really," I said.

"I thought about you every day I was gone," Spencer said through a fake smile. "I thought about crushing your head like a grape."

"I can't wait."

Before Spencer could say another word Mr. Groton appeared. "Is everything all right here?" he asked, putting his hand on my shoulder.

I felt Spencer's eyes on me. There was no way I was opening my mouth this time. Mr. Groton would have to suspend me first.

"Wyatt?" Mr. Groton asked. "Is everything okay?"

"Um, yup. We're just talking."

"That's good," said Mr. Groton, looking directly at Spencer. "Because my good friend Wayne Puckett was just asking about Mr. Randle. He wanted to know if you were staying out of trouble."

"Coach Puckett?" Spencer asked. "The high school football coach?"

"That's right," said Mr. Groton. "He told me he's looking forward to seeing you at tryouts this fall, but that he doesn't have any room on his team for discipline problems."

"What else did he say?" Spencer asked.

"He asked me to keep an eye on you. I promised I'd give him a full report on everything you do between now and the end of the school year."

Hearing that filled me with relief. I knew I'd be safe until the end of the year. Then it would be summer and I wouldn't see Spencer again until September, and by that time, I'd be a football player too.

I bet Spencer wouldn't even recognize me after one summer in the League of Pain.

Mr. Groton smiled at us. "All right, then. You boys get to class."

I ate lunch with Francis in Mr. Leland's classroom. The first thing I did was apologize for skipping the amateur tournament.

"It's cool," Francis said. "But you missed a good time. We were like five feet from the first tee, right up against the rope. I could hear the golfers talking to their caddies."

"That's awesome," I said, not thinking it was awesome at all.

Still, it did feel good to apologize for real, I thought as we helped Mr. Leland pack up his science equipment for the summer. "Where do you keep these?" I asked, pointing to the microscopes.

"I keep them in a secret storage room deep beneath the school," Mr. Leland said.

"Sounds like a good place to hide," Francis said.

I was relieved to see Francis joking around. If he was mad at me, he wasn't showing it. Maybe it would be better if I didn't say anything about the League of Pain or golf camp just yet.

Mr. Leland was stacking science books in a cardboard box. "So what are you two doing when school gets out?" he asked.

"We're going to golf camp," Francis replied, pointing at himself and me at the same time.

I tried to imagine what Francis was going to do when I didn't show up on the first day. Then I realized I had another problem. A humongous problem, actually. When it came to golf camp, I couldn't *not* say anything. If I just didn't show up, Francis would ask my mom where I was. That was if someone from the golf club didn't call her first. I needed a cover story that both of them would believe.

I wasn't sure how to create a cover story. If it had been a math problem, I would have used a formula. If it had been a history problem, I would have looked it up. This felt like a problem without a solution. But I knew every problem had a solution, so I used all my brain power to find one.

• • •

By Saturday morning, I still hadn't come up with anything. Hoping to give my mind a rest, I wandered into the den, where Dad was watching golf.

He patted the couch when he saw me. "Grab a seat," he said with a smile. "The final pair just teed off."

I sat down and tried to get interested. The golfer on the screen was standing on a bed of pine needles under a stand of oak trees. His ball lay on the ground, not far from the roots of the tree.

"What a jam!" the announcer was saying, like the guy was hanging off the edge of a cliff.

The golfer strolled from his ball to the fairway and back again. He talked to his caddy. He took a practice swing with one club, then replaced it with another club.

Dad shook his head. "He's overthinking it," he said. "If he just chips back to the fairway, he'll have a great look at the green. The problem is in the guy's head."

That made me think. Maybe my problem was all in my head. What if I just did the easy thing and asked Dad one more time, man to man, if I could play flag football instead of going to golf camp? It wasn't the League of Pain, but there would be no need for a cover story. Not a bad solution.

"I don't think I want to go to golf camp," I said, wincing as the words came out. It felt good to be honest with Dad, but I had no idea how he'd react.

Dad muted the television. "Maybe you don't now," he replied. "But once you get there and start swinging the clubs, you'll change your mind."

"Dad, I mean it," I said, gathering my courage. "I really want to play football with my friends. I don't want to go to golf camp. I know it's what you want, but it's not what I want."

"I thought we talked about this," Dad said. "The deal was you can try another sport after golf camp. I bet you'd be great at tennis."

"I've been playing football with some people from school," I said. "I even scored a touchdown. So can I play flag football? You just have to sign a permission slip, otherwise I can't do it."

I saw Dad's attention go back to the television screen, where a different golfer was standing in a sand trap. The guy stuck under the oak trees was gone.

"You mean later in the summer . . . after golf?"

Dad wasn't getting the message, and it was starting to make me mad. "*Instead* of golf," I said.

"Wyatt, I'm not going to tell you that you can't play football. That's your mom's call. But you are going to golf camp this summer. I know you don't believe me, but I really think golf is the perfect sport for you."

Why did that feel like an insult? Why couldn't Dad see that I didn't want to be the guy stuck in the sand trap? I wanted to be Brian Braun, who broke all the records and did whatever he wanted to do.

"I'm going upstairs," I told Dad.

"Wyatt," he called.

Something in the way his voice had softened hinted

at a change of heart. I stopped on the steps and listened hopefully.

"Yeah?"

"By the end of the summer, you'll be thanking me for this. I promise." Then he winked.

That was the end of the conversation.

I went into my room, closed the door behind me, and dialed the phone. I didn't have a cover story yet, so I just started talking.

"Pilchuck Golf and Tennis Club," said a woman's voice on the other end of the line. "Jo speaking."

"Uh, hi," I said.

"Hello," said the woman. "How can I help you?"

"My name is Wyatt Parker. I'm signed up for golf camp this summer."

"Are you confirming your place?"

"No, I, uh, have to cancel. I just found out that I have to go to, um, space camp."

"I'm sorry to hear you won't be at golf camp. Just so you know, the prepaid fee is nonrefundable. That's club policy."

"That's okay," I said.

"Great," said the woman. "Is there anything else I can help you with?"

"Nope."

"Then have a nice day, Wyatt. And have fun at space camp."

The second I hung up the phone, Kate pushed my door open. She was holding a piece of paper with math problems on it.

"Thanks for knocking," I told her.

"Why did you say you were going to space camp?" she asked, marching into my room.

"Once again, it's none of your business."

"Tell me, or I'll tell Mom and Dad, and then it will be everybody's business."

CHAPTER THIRTEEN

Kate and I stood in the center of the room, staring at each other as Aaron's music thumped against the walls next door. I knew she wouldn't actually tell on me and I was pretty sure she knew that too. But I also had to face the fact that it wouldn't take Kate long to figure out I wasn't going to golf camp, or space camp. Then she'd really start asking questions.

I sat on the edge of my bed. "Can you keep a secret?" I asked Kate. I had to make sure, especially before telling her the truth about my plans, except for the part about Aaron being the one who told me about the League of Pain in the first place. Of course it took her less than a second to put that together anyway.

"I knew Aaron wasn't volunteering this summer!" she exclaimed.

"Who said anything about Aaron?" I said, trying to play dumb. "This has nothing to do with him."

"Oh, please," Kate shot back. "Who would ever believe that story about him picking up trash in the park? Plus, duh, it's football."

"Good point," I said. "So you won't say anything to Mom and Dad?"

"I won't say anything," Kate said. "But you have to help me with my math homework."

"What am I, the family tutor?" I grumbled. "How come nobody in this house can do their own homework?"

"Please, Wyatt," she begged. "It's just one little worksheet. It's not even homework. It's just practice for my test."

"Mom told you to do your own homework."

"Mom told you not to play football."

"Fine," I said. "Sit down and grab a pencil. I'm not doing this for you."

"This is so cool," Kate said, her eyes shining. "It's just like *Don't Tell Mom I'm a Mermaid*. Only instead of being a mermaid, you're trying to play football. And instead of me helping you get back to the ocean, you're helping me with math."

For the next half hour, I showed Kate how to multiply and divide fractions. It didn't take long for her to pick it up. When it came to brains, she was closer to me than Aaron was. As soon as we finished her worksheet, she went right back to explaining the plot of *Don't Tell Mom I'm a Mermaid*.

"See, the only people who knew the main character was a mermaid were the mermaid's friends, and they all had to keep the secret from their parents and teachers because if any adult found out, she'd die."

"Wait, her mom didn't know her own kid was a mermaid?" I asked, handing the finished worksheet back to Kate. "That doesn't make sense."

"It makes sense, Wyatt. There's a lot Mom doesn't know about me," she replied secretively.

"Fine," I said. "How did they keep the secret?"

"First, they took an oath. So you, Aaron, and I will have to do that. Second, they came up with code names, built hideouts, and even made up a language only they understood. So we'll have to do that too."

"How about we just start with the oath?"

Kate sighed. "Okay, but if we get busted speaking English, don't blame me."

It took us a while to get Aaron's attention because he was on the phone with Olivia. Finally he came into my room looking seriously annoyed.

"What?" he asked.

"She knows," I said.

"Knows what?"

"About the League of Pain," said Kate, savoring the moment.

Aaron picked up my paperback copy of *Frankenstein* and hurled it at me. "What did I say about keeping your mouth shut?" he barked.

"She figured it out," I replied, covering my face in case another book was coming at me. "She's not going to tell anyone."

"Wyatt's the mermaid," said Kate.

"The what?" Aaron asked.

"Never mind," I said, then looked at Kate. "Can we get this over with?"

Aaron glared at me, like he knew something weird was about to happen. "Get what over with?"

"We have to take an oath," said Kate.

"Do I look like a Boy Scout?" Aaron said. "I'm not taking an oath."

"You have to, or they'll find out, and the mermaid will die."

"Who will find out? And what mermaid?" Aaron looked around. "What is going on here?"

Kate held out her hand, palm down. I put my hand on hers. Reluctantly, Aaron did the same.

"Now what?" he asked.

"Now we swear the mermaid oath that will bind us together for all time," Kate explained in a hushed voice. "Repeat after me," she started. "Under sea, under sky, under star, under—"

"Oh-kay," said Aaron, pulling his hand away. "How about we cut out all this sea and sky garbage and get to the point." His eyes shifted between me and Kate. "If either of you tell anybody about the League of Pain, I'll drive you into the mountains and leave you where nobody will ever find you. Deal?"

"Deal," I said.

"That's not how it goes," said Kate.

"Just say 'deal,' " I said.

"Fine." Kate sighed. "Deal."

"Is that it?" Aaron asked.

"Hold on," I said. "So Mom and Dad think I'll be at golf camp. The golf club thinks I'll be at space camp—"

Aaron interrupted me. "Space camp? Seriously?"

"It's all I could think of. The point is, they won't be expecting me at golf camp."

"So what's the problem?"

"The problem is this story has major holes," I said, starting to panic. "Like, what happens if Dad drops by to play a few rounds and I'm not there? What do I say after two weeks when I'm not any better at golf? We have to think this through or it's not going to work."

"Relax," said Aaron. "Lying isn't about thinking

it through. Lying is about thinking on your feet. You have to take it one problem at a time and survive to live another day. There's just one rule: once you start lying, don't stop."

Kate jumped in. "Oh, like in gym class Friday, Madison asked me if I liked her haircut and I said I did, and when she asked me if I liked her shoes I said I liked those too even though I thought they were both ugly."

"Sure, whatever," said Aaron, heading for the door. "Just don't start anything you can't finish."

"I think it's too late for that," I said as Aaron and Kate left my room.

Even though I knew I was taking a big risk defying Mom and Dad for the first time, I fell asleep easily that night, knowing my secret would be safe. Aaron had never given me a reason to trust him, but this time none of us could say anything to Mom and Dad without all of us getting in trouble. We were bound together for all eternity, just like Kate wanted.

CHAPTER FOURTEEN

The next morning I called McKlusky, who told me there was another two-hand-touch game in the park at noon. After breakfast, I snuck out of the house without saying goodbye and rode my bike to Boardman Park, arriving just in time for kickoff. It was the last Sunday before the end of the school year, and my final chance to practice before the League of Pain started.

For most of the game I ran downfield on every play, hoping someone would throw me the ball. I was just beginning to wonder if I'd ever get to do anything else when Caleb called my number in the huddle. At the time, we were near midfield and the score was tied 35–35. But it was fourth down.

"What do you want to do?" Caleb asked. "We could go for it, but if we don't score and they do, they win."

"And we have to score on this play," Kenny replied. "It's fourth down and we can't get two completions on one throw."

"I say we go for it," said Caleb.

"Let me guess," said Khalil. "Fake it, then throw to Morelli."

Caleb shook his head. "They'll be expecting that. We need to shake it up." He looked at me. "Can you catch?" he asked.

"I think so," I said.

"Good," said Caleb, holding out his palm. "You line up next to Roy like this." He poked the right side of his palm with two fingers. "Run side by side for about twenty yards. When you're downfield, Roy, you gun it for the end zone. The defense will follow you. Wyatt, when you see Roy speed up, you cut across the field. I'll hit you in stride."

"Then what do I do?" I asked.

Caleb turned his hand over. "Catch the ball and follow your blockers to the promised land."

I walked up to the line of scrimmage ready to play football. For the first time that day, I felt like I was in the game. I lined up beside Roy and ran as fast as I could to keep up with him. After about twenty yards, he accelerated straight down the sideline. That was when I broke left and crossed the field. Out of the corner of my eye, I could see Raj had left me alone to cover Roy. I was wide open!

Suddenly the football was coming right toward me. Instinctively I held up my hands and caught it without slowing down. Tucking the ball into my arm the way I'd seen the pros do on TV, I turned and raced toward our end zone. I knew I'd have to hurry. Fish and Raj were all the way on the other side of the field, but McKlusky was coming up behind me and he had much longer legs than I did.

I felt the wind at my back. And just like in the baseball game, I kept myself focused and knew nothing was going to stop me from getting where I had to go. With a burst of speed, I broke away from McKlusky. I wasn't in the clear, though. Raj was zeroing in on me from the side. He reached me just as I got to the goal line. As he extended his arms to tag me, his fingers less than an inch from my shoulders, I planted my right foot and spun around him. Raj flew right past me, stumbling out of bounds as I sprinted into the end zone for a touchdown.

"Touchdown!" I heard Caleb yell. He was jumping up and down with his fists in the air.

I couldn't believe it. I'd won the game. It felt just as good as it had in baseball.

Roy scooped up the football and stuck it in Fish's face. "Better luck next time, losers!" he shouted before throwing the ball in the air.

Kenny high-fived me. "What a move!" he said. "That was amazing."

"I told him he should play football," McKlusky said to Kenny as we picked up the cones and sweatshirts before leaving the field.

Soon we were walking down Boardman Street under a bright blue sky. The sun cast long shadows of Kenny, McKlusky, Caleb, and me as we left the park behind us. There was a lot of friendly shoving and tackling, especially for whoever happened to be holding the football at the moment. I was having so much fun being part of the pack, I didn't even mind when the three of them knocked down the bike I'd been pushing and dog-piled me on a grassy corner. I couldn't remember the last time I had laughed that hard hanging out with Francis.

"It's too bad you can't play flag football with us this summer," said McKlusky when we were standing in front of my house.

Something about the way McKlusky said that made me feel like I was officially a part of their group. But that left me wishing more than ever that I could play football with them this summer. It sounded safer for one thing, and would probably be more fun. There was nothing I could do, though, since Mom and Dad were not going to change their minds.

"Hey, maybe we can just keep playing two-hand touch," I said hopefully, wondering why nobody had thought of that before. We could be like our own league, except without the pain.

McKlusky shook his head. "Never gonna happen," he said. "My parents said I gotta do an organized activity. You know, supervised."

"Same here," said Caleb, nodding. "Otherwise they think I'm just wasting time."

"They don't realize they're just wasting money," Kenny added. "We could be playing football for free."

For a second I wondered if I should tell them about the League of Pain, but I knew Aaron would consider that a betrayal, so I stayed quiet. I hoped I'd still be a part of the group when summer ended.

• • •

The smell of barbecue drifted into my backyard as Evan stood in the middle of the grass holding Kate's purple hula hoop. There was a jump rope tied to it. "Pretend you're drowning," she said. "I'll save you."

"Okay," I said. "I'm drowning."

I was actually sitting on the porch step.

"Wyatt, help me out. I need to practice my rescue technique. So get down here and drown." She pointed to the grass.

I lay down on the lawn.

"Flop around," Evan ordered.

I flopped around.

"Now call for help."

"Help. I'm drowning. Help."

"Relax!" Evan shouted. "I'm a lifeguard. Do not struggle. Hold on to this flotation ring and I will pull you to the side of the pool."

She threw the hula hoop. It landed an arm's length away from me. I wrapped my arms around it and Evan pretended to pull me forward. She knelt down and turned me onto my back. She then held her ear to my mouth. "Yep, you're breathing." Leaning in, she asked, "What's your name?"

"George Washington," I said.

"And you're responsive," she replied, nodding. "You're going to be okay. I better check your pulse just to be sure."

I lay still on the grass while Evan picked up my arm and held my wrist in her fingers. We weren't holding hands, but it was close.

"Your heart rate is a little high," she said after about ten seconds.

I sat up. "Well, I did almost drown."

"True," she answered, sitting next to me. "That

must have been scary. Lucky for you there was a lifeguard on duty."

"You know who else could have saved me?"

Evan plucked a blade of grass. "Who?"

"Dr. Pirate."

"I wouldn't let someone with a hook take my pulse. That could get bloody."

I wondered if she'd hold hands with someone who had a hook. Maybe in *Dr. Pirate 2*, Dr. Pirate would get a girlfriend and they could hold hooks. "I think I want to go to the fireworks with you," I blurted out.

"Cool," Evan answered. "You don't have to fold flags with the old folks?"

"I guess all the flags are already folded."

"Well, look for us at the very top of the hill, by the sundial." Evan stood up to go. "I'll be the one dressed in red, white, and blue."

"I think a lot of people will be."

"That's a joke, Wyatt."

"Oh, ha."

She smiled. "I should have let you drown."

"You'll make a great lifeguard someday," I told her. "I mean it. That's not a joke."

"Thanks. I hope no kids fall into the deep end on my first day, though."

"Wyatt," Mom called from the kitchen. "I need you to come inside and try on some pants."

"Mom, it's too warm for pants," I said.

Mom appeared on the porch holding a pair of brown dress pants on a hanger. "I need to know if these fit you because if they don't, I need to buy you new pants for your graduation on Wednesday."

Taking the pants from Mom, I said good night to Evan and went inside.

"Toodle-oo, kangaroo," she said as the door closed behind me.

CHAPTER FIFTEEN

After the graduation ceremony Wednesday, there was a party in the school courtyard for the families. Mom and Dad made me pose for a million photographs. When that was over, I sat in the shade on a folding chair with a glass of lemonade and a sugar cookie.

Francis showed up and took a seat next to me. Sipping the last of my lemonade, I realized it was now or never. I had to tell him I wasn't going to golf camp.

"I'm so glad we're out of here." Francis sighed and adjusted his tie. "No more kid stuff." All the other guys had taken their ties off, or at least loosened them, but not Francis. His was still hanging tight and straight. "Our new lives start this summer," he added. "I can't wait to be around people who—"

"I have some bad news," I said, cutting Francis off. "I can't go to golf camp with you."

"Seriously?" Francis said. "Why not?"

I looked around like we were being watched. "It's the stock market," I whispered.

"What about it?"

"All I know is my dad said no more golf camp."

Francis shook his head. "Man, I told him to diversify his portfolio."

"Well, it's too late now," I said, trying to act as bummed as Francis.

"Do you want my dad to talk to him? Maybe he could throw a few tips his way."

"No!" I practically shouted. "You can't say anything to your parents." I lowered my voice again. "My dad is kind of embarrassed, and if your parents knew I wasn't in golf camp, they might start asking questions."

"Okay," said Francis, nodding. "I'll cover for you. But I don't know what I'll say if you're not in the father-son tournament."

"I'll come up with something by then," I said, tossing my empty cup into a nearby trash can.

"What are you going to do instead?" he asked.

"Probably just lie low."

"Hey," Francis said, excitement returning to his

voice. "I have a great idea. You could be my caddy. I could pay you."

I didn't think it was possible, but Francis actually managed to find something that sounded less fun than golf camp. I tried to picture myself lugging his clubs up and down the fairway while he soaked up the sunshine. "I'll think about it," I said. "But thanks for having my back."

"What are friends for?" Francis replied, holding out his fist, which I bumped with mine.

I felt a twinge of guilt as our knuckles met. It was hard to forget that I was lying to someone I liked. Still, I thought I had a right to do what I wanted this summer. I just wished I could have been honest about it with Francis. That was impossible, though. If Francis knew what I was really doing, he would make it his job to tell his parents, or my parents, even if it got me in trouble. So it was really *his* fault I had to make up the stock market story. It had to be this way, which was never the fun way.

• • •

"We're so proud of you, Wyatt," Mom said as she handed me a gift-wrapped box with an envelope taped to the outside. It was dinnertime after graduation, and the whole family was watching me.

"What is this?" I asked.

"It's a lot of things," Dad replied. "It's your graduation present slash starting-golf-camp present slash, well, just all-around-great-job present."

"Do I get a present?" Kate asked. "I got good grades too."

Yeah, thanks to me, I thought.

"So he got good grades?" Aaron said. "Why do we have to make a big deal out of it?"

"It's called positive reinforcement, pal," Dad told Aaron. "You want presents at dinner? You bring home straight As and stay out of trouble for a year, I'll get you whatever you want."

"I want a truck," Aaron said.

Dad looked at him. "You get straight As, I'll buy you a truck. Until then, be happy for your brother. If you're nice to him, he might tell you some of his secrets."

"Yeah, Wyatt," Aaron said. "Tell me some of your secrets. What makes you so smart and special?"

I wanted to crawl under the table until the end of dinner. Why did Mom and Dad have to make such a big deal about my grades in front of Aaron?

Mom pointed at the box. "Open it up," she said.

I felt the box. It was pretty obvious the present was a pair of shoes, or at least something heavy in a shoe box. Sure enough, when I'd pulled off all the wrapping paper, I was staring at a pair of golf shoes. A pair of old golf shoes. I could tell they'd been white when they were new, but grass and dirt stains had turned them a brownish green on the sides. Metal spikes jutted out from the bottom of each shoe.

"For golf camp!" Mom exclaimed, in case I couldn't put it together myself. "They were your dad's."

"I've held on to them so I could pass them on to one of you. They've been in this box for thirty years."

"That's gross," said Kate.

"So, they're yours now," Dad went on. "Just in time too. Camp starts Monday, right?"

I nodded. "Yup," I said. For some kids, anyway.

"Do you like them?" Mom asked.

"They're great," I said.

"The best thing is they're all broken in. You could run a marathon in those shoes."

"They have spikes," I pointed out.

"Well, a marathon on grass," Dad admitted.

Mom began clearing the dishes. "You're going to have so much fun at golf camp, Wyatt."

That made me wince. Every time Mom or Dad mentioned golf camp, it was like being pricked by a pin. When I thought of my double life as an adventure in which I had to outsmart everyone to stay alive, it was exciting. But when I remembered that I was flat-out lying to my friends and family, it felt a little less fun. I just hoped Mom and Dad wouldn't find out the truth before summer even started.

I looked across the table at Aaron. I was pretty sure he wouldn't say anything. After all, I knew a secret about him too. And Kate wouldn't talk either. Not after the mermaid oath.

"There's more good news," Mom announced, coming back to the table with a plate of cookies. "Kate and Dad are going shopping tomorrow for golf clubs."

"What?" Aaron asked, looking more outraged than ever. "Why? What did she do?"

"She got a B-plus on her math test," Dad said, tousling Kate's hair as he passed by her chair. "Your mom was so proud she even had it framed. Show 'em, Ellen."

Smiling, Mom reached under her chair and revealed a framed sheet of paper. It had a giant *B+* on the top next to Kate's name, and a dozen completed math problems. "Great job, sweetie," said Mom, hugging Kate.

"Wyatt helped me a little," Kate admitted.

"You're a good big brother," Mom said, reaching across the table to pat my hand.

I hoped she'd remember that if the truth about this summer ever got out.

CHAPTER SIXTEEN

Summer vacation was finally here. I had survived the school year, but only because Mr. Groton had threatened to ruin Spencer's football career if he bothered me. Now I was on my own again. If Spencer found me over the summer, I would have to protect myself. Luckily, it was also the time for the League of Pain—and if that wasn't going to make me tough enough to face Spencer, nothing would. Aaron had already told me we'd play every weekday between now and the Fourth of July, the day of the championship game. That meant thirteen days of football and then, fireworks.

Brushing my teeth after breakfast, I noticed Aaron

was wearing beat-up cargo shorts and a T-shirt with dirt stains. I found clothes in my room that looked like his, threw them on, and went out into the hallway.

"What are you doing?" Aaron asked. "You can't go downstairs dressed like that."

"Why not?"

"Because you're supposed to be going to a golf course," he said, slapping me on the side of the head. "You have to wear something nice."

Looking down at my grass-stained clothes, I realized Aaron was right. For a guy who didn't know a right triangle from a trapezoid, he sure could think through a lie. "Thanks," I said. "I'll go change."

"But bring those with you," he added. "Or you'll trash your golf clothes."

"Obviously," I agreed, grabbing a wad of money from the peanut butter jar in case I got hungry after the game.

In the driveway a few minutes later, I tied the laces of my golf shoes together, threw them over my neck, and said goodbye to Mom.

Dad was starting up his car in the driveway with Kate in the backseat. "You sure you don't want a ride to the golf course?" he asked. "It's not far out of my way."

"I'll ride my bike," I said.

Dad started to drive away, then stopped suddenly and looked back. "Wait," he said. "Don't I need to sign you in?"

"Francis said if you're over fourteen you can sign yourself in," I said.

"Okay," Dad replied. "Well, I can't wait to hear all about it tonight. You know where to pick up your clubs when you get there?"

"Yup," I said.

He pointed to the shoes as he drove off. "Take care of those."

I forced a smile as I strapped the shoes carefully to the rack of my bike so I wouldn't have to tell Dad I'd lost them on my first day.

"See you at the club," Kate called, her head sticking out of the window as Dad drove away.

The wind rushed over my helmet as I sailed down the hill toward the park. In my head I went over the directions to the field Aaron had given me last night: go in the main entrance and follow the gravel trail until it turns into dirt. Stay on the dirt trail all the way through the ravine. Look for the break in the blackberry bushes. Listen for voices.

I followed Aaron's directions to a grassy area hidden between a row of pine trees and the side of a dusty hill. I stood alone in the middle of the field, staring all around me. It was impossible to see the outside world. It was like being at the bottom of a bowl. At one end of the bowl, two oak trees about fifty feet apart reached toward each other with their longest branches. Turning around, I saw two boulders on the other end about the same distance apart sitting in front of a thick mess of blackberry bushes. I bet those were the end zones.

But where was everyone else?

Then I heard a noise from the other side of the hill. Like a flock of birds mixed with a stampede of horses all in the middle of an earthquake. As it got louder, it began to sound more human and I could make out voices. Well, not voices exactly. More like deranged yelling and screaming.

A dust cloud formed at the top of the hill as heads began to appear. A second later the heads were whole bodies. Big bodies racing and tumbling straight down the dirt hill toward me with their arms in the air. As they reached level ground, I picked up only one word coming from the pack: "FOOOTBAAALLLL!"

Suddenly I was surrounded by ten, maybe fifteen heavyset guys with jerseys, arms as big as my thighs, and cleats. None of them seemed to notice me. They jumped into one another, stomping across the field and beating their chests.

As they stormed around me like wild things, I could see that some of them had streaks of mud painted under their eyes.

I was never going to get out of Boardman Park alive.

Soon they had stopped moving long enough for me to make out a few faces, and the first person I recognized nearly sent me running for the golf course. Standing before me, with his pasty, jiggly arms hanging out of a sleeveless shirt, was the last guy I wanted to see: Spencer Randle.

"I don't believe it," Spencer said. He was out of breath, red in the face, and already sweating. Streaks of dirt lined his cheeks. "You're not here to play football, are you?"

I looked up at Spencer, too shocked to speak. He had a gleam in his eye like he had just won a million dollars in the lottery. What he had really won was a chance to hurt me every day without any chance of getting in trouble. What coach would get mad at a player for injuring someone in a football game?

Aaron appeared beside me. Was this the moment when my brother would finally do something to protect me? Looking Spencer in the eye, he said, "If you get a shot at him, take it. But keep it clean. You know the rules." Then he walked away.

"There's nobody here to protect you," Spencer said, pointing back at Aaron. "Out here, it's every man for himself."

"Aren't we on teams?" I asked.

Spencer didn't answer right away. "Just be ready for pain," he said finally.

A moment later a loud voice rose above the others. "Game time!"

I couldn't see over the bodies that stood like trees all around me. So I just listened.

"Same teams as last year," I heard. "Same rules as always. Right?"

"Right!" everyone shouted.

"Cool," the voice said. "Rookies up front."

I saw three or four guys make their way toward the front of the pack. Then I felt two hands shove me from behind.

"That means you," Aaron said.

I made my way to the open space where the other rookies were standing. I recognized three of them from my baseball team: Julian, Luther, and Shane. Those three had picked on me all spring. Now that we were all rookies in the League of Pain, they didn't seem so scary. In fact, they looked more scared than I was.

Nearby was a guy who towered over everyone. He stared at me. "Are you kidding?" he said to nobody in particular. "Is this a joke? Who brought the hobbit?"

Everyone laughed.

"He's with me, Herc," Aaron said to the big guy.

Herc shook his head. "He's too small. He's gonna

get hurt and then someone's gonna find out about us. He's out."

"He's just a sub," Aaron said.

Wait a minute, I thought. *Did he just call me a sub? What was that about?*

Herc gave up. "Fine, let the little guy stand on the sideline," he said to Aaron. "But he's on your team. Go with José."

Aaron opened his mouth to say something, but Herc had turned away. Luther and I were put on Aaron's team. Julian and Shane went to Spencer's team. Then it was time to play.

I walked with Aaron to the other side of the field for the kickoff. We followed José, who had the biggest muscles I had ever seen in real life. They looked like grapefruits popping out of his arms.

"Why did you say I was a sub?" I asked Aaron.

"You didn't think you were going to show up and play on the first day, did you?" he answered. "You gotta wait for your spot."

"But you said I was in the league."

"Yeah, as a sub."

"When do I get to play?" I asked, feeling a little relieved, but also annoyed. I'd gone through a lot of trouble to get there, and even though I was genuinely scared for my life, I still wanted to be a part of the action this summer.

"When someone else stops playing," Aaron replied,

kicking rocks off the field as we followed José and the rest of our team.

"So how does this work?" I asked, jogging behind Aaron. "Do we pick different teams every week?"

"No," Aaron answered. "This is your team. You're an Idiot."

"What do you mean?"

"That's our team name. We're the Idiots. They're the Morons. Don't ask me who came up with those names because I have no idea and nobody does."

"We just play each other every day?"

"Yup."

"What are we playing for? I mean, is there a trophy or anything?"

"Trophy? No, there's no trophy. There's just knowing you were league champions."

"But there's only two teams."

"So you're either first or last. Now quit asking me questions."

I didn't really see what was so special about being the champions of a league nobody had ever heard of that had only two teams anyway.

"What are the rules?" I asked.

"The rules are the rules of football," Aaron said. He looked over at me as the Morons lined up, ready to kick off. "Go stand over there with the other rookie," he ordered, pointing at Luther. "The game's about to start."

I stood on the sideline with Luther and watched as Aaron caught the kickoff and started running upfield. José and a couple of other guys formed a wall in front of Aaron, but Spencer and his team ran through it like it was made of paper. Aaron disappeared under a pile of bodies. One by one, players from both teams jumped on the stack. When Aaron crawled out from the heap, his shirt was torn and his face was bright red. He was shaking out his hand and grimacing.

"Someone stepped on my fingers," he said. He looked up and smiled. "Man, I love football."

José pulled the team together into a huddle close to the sideline. There were five guys on the field: Aaron, José, Derek, and two guys who looked like they each weighed more than my whole family.

I saw José glance around the huddle. "All right, here's the play. Twenty-two falcon on three. You Idiots know what to do?"

Everyone said yes and José seemed satisfied. He slapped his hands together; then the guys all got into position. One of the big ones crouched in front of José.

"Hut, hut-hut, *hike*!" he barked.

And it was on. The Idiots and Morons crashed into one another like two herds of elephants. It was nothing like the two-hand-touch games with McKlusky and Raj. I heard grunting, growling, and cries of

125

pain rising above the sound of bodies colliding. Now I could see why Spencer was so happy to see me. Anywhere else, this would have been a crime. Here it was just part of the game.

Luther and I sat in the dirt on the sideline and watched the Idiots and Morons crash and bash, play after play, until they were filthy with mud, sweat, and blood. The longer I watched, the more comfortable I was with being a spectator. I had come to the field to play football, but now I wasn't so sure. Secretly, a part of me was relieved to be a sub.

"Man," Luther muttered. "I hope someone comes out soon. I'm getting bored."

But I couldn't see anybody who seemed ready to come out of the game. For every skinned knee, bloody knuckle, and jammed finger, I also saw a lot of laughing, smiling, and high fives. I couldn't tell if they were ignoring the pain, or enjoying it.

As it turned out, Luther got his wish a few plays later when Derek had to leave the game, and not by choice.

Derek, who was my age but almost as tall as Aaron, caught a short pass from José in the middle of the field. He took two steps before running into Herc's shoulder, nose first. Derek wobbled backward, stumbling over his own feet, and landed on his butt. He sat, squinting so hard his eyes nearly disappeared under his forehead. Blood began to trickle out of his right nostril.

"I'm okay," he said, bobbing his head and wiping his nose with his sleeve.

"Dude, you're not okay," José told him. "Take a break. Come back in when you stop bleeding."

Derek didn't argue with José. I had a feeling nobody did. He trudged to the sideline and sat down next to me and Luther.

My heart began to beat faster as I realized what this meant. I might be going into the game after all!

José pointed at Luther. "You!" he called. "You're in."

"Yes!" cried Luther, leaping to his feet and dashing onto the field, momentarily losing his footing halfway to the huddle.

Phew, I thought. Luther would be the first rookie in the game. I'd watch what he did, and whatever he did wrong, I'd do the opposite. If someone else needed a break later in the day, I'd step in, ready to play. Until then I'd cheer for Luther and the rest of the Idiots.

Except Luther wasn't heading into the game. He was hobbling back to the sideline.

CHAPTER SEVENTEEN

"Looks like you're in," said Luther, pointing to his ankle. "Twisted it pretty bad."

I looked over at Derek, who was reclining against a log, staring at the trees, waiting for his nose to stop bleeding.

"Let's go, rookie!" José yelled.

I stood up, shook the dirt off my shorts, and hurried to the huddle.

"Welcome to the game," said José. "I'm José, the quarterback."

"Call me Planet," said one of the big dudes.

"Ox," said the other. "We're the offensive line," he added, gesturing to himself and Planet.

"You know me," said Aaron. "I'm the wide receiver. I catch passes and score touchdowns."

"Only because I get the ball in your hands, pretty boy," said José.

"And only because we block for José," said Planet, gesturing to himself and Ox.

"So what can you do?" Ox asked.

"I'm pretty fast," I said. "Maybe I can be the running back."

"You think you can run through them?" Aaron asked, pointing to the other team.

I took one look at Spencer and Herc and realized Aaron had a point. Julian was the smallest guy on the Morons and even he was bigger than me.

"I tell you what," said José. "Why don't you run some slant routes underneath? Maybe the defense will lose you in the crowd. Cool?"

"Okay," I said.

"In that case," said José, "it's twenty-one falcon on two. Got it?"

Planet, Ox, and Aaron nodded confidently as we broke out of the huddle.

"Where do I go?"

"Just stand here," José said, walking me to a space a few feet to the right of Aaron. "When Ox hikes it to me, run diagonally and look for the football. If I throw it to you, catch it."

129

José jogged back to the center, leaving me face to face with Julian.

"Looks like I drew the *short* straw," he said, with a familiar look on his face. It was the look that said he knew he was bigger, faster, and stronger than me, and there was nothing I could do about it. I used to see it every day when we were on the same baseball team.

But now it was different. Because compared to Spencer Randle and the other Morons, Julian was a shrimp. It almost made me laugh to think that I was ever afraid of him.

A few seconds later, Ox snapped the ball to José, starting the play. I darted ahead five feet, pushing past Julian before turning in toward midfield. Julian tried to follow me but got screened by Aaron coming in the other direction.

My worst fear had come true on the first play. I was wide open. I looked back at José. He spotted me. I saw his arm go back and he released the ball. It was coming toward me like a bullet, but so was something else, something bigger. I glanced up to see Spencer charging at me with his head down. I forgot all about the football. I hit the deck like I was ducking a fireball.

When I opened my eyes, Spencer was staring at me. "Boo," he said, laughing. Then his face went cold. "Next time I'm going to let you catch it," he whispered. "So I can blow you up."

I got a lot of dirty looks back in the huddle. José didn't pay attention to me after that. Even if he had thrown it to me, I don't think I would have caught it. I was too worried about Spencer. I always knew he was out there, waiting for a chance to lay me out as soon as I had the football.

The Morons won that day, 35–28. I walked away from the field wondering if I should just quit. But Aaron caught up to me. "You better find a way to play better," he said. "Because that was embarrassing. I can't believe you intentionally fell down so you wouldn't get tackled."

"Gimme a break," I said. "It was my first play."

"That's no excuse."

"What did you want me to do?" I asked. "He was going to crush me. When you think about it, I was actually doing the best thing for the team. I mean, if I get hurt, what are we going to do? There's nobody left on the sideline. Derek and Luther are both hurt."

"The way you played, we'd be better off with four guys instead of five," Aaron said, grabbing his backpack and heading for the trail that led away from the field.

"Wait," I said. "Where are you going?"

"To the corner of It's None of Your Business and Don't Follow Me. Have you heard of it?"

"Where am I supposed to go?"

"Don't know, don't care," Aaron replied. "But you might want to get those shorts cleaned."

I looked down and saw right away what Aaron meant. I had forgotten to change out of my nice shorts for golf!

It was only a few minutes after twelve, which meant I had four hours to kill before I could show up at home without Mom or Dad asking questions. At least that left me with plenty of time to find some clean shorts. Taking the side streets in case Mom was doing errands in town, I rode my bike to the Laundromat on Verlot Street, where I changed into my football shorts and tossed the dirty ones into a washing machine, which cost all the money I had with me. I didn't want to sit around in the Laundromat for an hour, so I went down the street to the library, where I checked out a book called *Golf for Everyone*. I spent the rest of the afternoon doing what I did best, studying. Only instead of equations, it was how to swing a golf club.

Dad was in the garage when I coasted down the driveway. "There he is!" he said. "How was the first day of golf camp?"

"Great," I said, reciting what I had read in *Golf for Everyone*. "We worked on our grips. They also

132

taught us how to shift our weight when we swing. We didn't really get to do any putting, though."

"You will," Dad said. "I promise."

I knew I wasn't telling Dad the truth, but it didn't feel like lying. It felt like telling him what he wanted to hear so he'd be happy. That made it easier for me.

• • •

At the start of dinner, Aaron reached over me and grabbed a burger off the serving plate in the middle of the table.

"What happened to your hand?" Mom asked him. "Did you hurt it volunteering?"

"Um, yep," Aaron said, looking at his hand.

"How did that happen?" Mom looked concerned.

"Well, this other volunteer was trying to lift the lid on the storage shed where all the tools are kept. I went over to help him and just as I stuck my hand in there, the lid slipped and landed on it. I can move it fine, so I know it's not broken." Aaron forced a smile. "You don't have to sue or anything."

"El," Dad said to Mom. "Did you sign any paperwork for this? There must have been an insurance waiver."

Mom shook her head. "Aaron, is there anything we need to sign?"

"I'll ask tomorrow," Aaron said.

"Does anyone want to know about my day?" Kate asked, waving her fork in the air.

"Of course, sweetie," said Mom. "How was your first day of golf camp?"

"Really, really great," said Kate. "My coach, her name is Terri, is so nice and she told me I was a natural, which I guess is true."

"Did you see Wyatt?" Mom asked.

I held my breath, but Kate didn't miss a beat. "Only once," she said. "His group was walking from the putting green to the driving range, but he was too far away."

"Sounds like everyone's summer is off to a great start," said Dad, smiling. "I can't wait to hear what happens tomorrow."

After one day split between the League of Pain and the Pilchuck Laundromat, I had to agree with Dad. This was going to be a summer to remember.

CHAPTER EIGHTEEN

The next day I was back in the game. "Derek's mom found his bloody clothes and signed him up for art camp," José explained. "And Luther twisted his ankle. You ready to step up?"

"Um, I guess so."

José put his face right into mine. "Man, there's no 'I guess so' in this league. It's either yes or no. So which is it? Are you ready to step up?"

"Yes," I said.

José nodded. "That's better."

On our first drive, we had the ball and were on the move, going no-huddle, which meant José was calling the plays from the line of scrimmage.

He looked down at Aaron, who stood at one end of the line. "Thirty-one eagle on three!" José shouted, scanning the defense. Spencer and Bunyon were creeping forward. Suddenly José raised his voice even louder. "Stampede! Stampede! Stampede!"

I had no idea what thirty-one eagle or stampede meant, so I just ran straight ahead as fast as I could. One of the Morons blew past me going in the other direction.

Behind me, I heard two thuds and suddenly everyone started running toward the line of scrimmage.

"Ball's out!" I heard Bunyon yell.

I turned around to see José lying on his side with Spencer on top of him. Both teams were chasing after the football, which was bouncing away like a frightened rabbit. I watched as Julian scooped it up and ran for an easy touchdown.

José picked himself up and marched over to me. "What did I say?" he barked.

"About what?"

"Did you hear me call the play?"

"Yeah, but—"

"Did you hear me say stampede?"

"Yeah, but—"

"What does stampede mean?"

"I don't know," I admitted. "Nobody told me."

José grabbed Aaron by the collar. "Did you teach him the calls?"

"I was going to, but—"

José glared at Aaron. "You brought him here. It's your job to teach him the calls." Then he looked at me again, a little calmer now. "Stampede means blitz. You know what a blitz is, right?"

"When the defense rushes the quarterback," I said, remembering what Roy Morelli had taught me in the two-hand-touch game.

"Right. When the other team blitzes, you have to help block. If they send four guys, Planet and Ox can't stop all of them. Got it?"

"Yeah, I got it."

José had one more word for Aaron. "He better know everything by tomorrow."

Aaron and I stood in the middle of the field after the game ended and everyone else had left. "Listen up," he said. "I'm going to tell you what you need to know and you better not forget it."

"I've been getting straight As since second grade," I said. "I think I can remember a few plays."

"I hope so," Aaron said angrily. "Because if I get on José's bad side, I'm done."

"Hey, don't yell at me," I said. "It's not my fault José's mad at you. You were supposed to tell me this before we played."

"Look, it's pretty simple," Aaron went on. "You already know that stampede means blitz. When you hear that, stay near the quarterback and block anyone who's trying to sack him."

"What does thirty-one eagle mean?"

"The first number José calls is always for me. The second number is always for you. The three means I'm supposed to run a slant route. The one means you run a curl. If he calls a number with a two in it, that means a post route."

"One for curl, two for post, three for slant," I said. "What does eagle mean?"

"When you hear an animal that can fly, that's a pass. Anything that can't fly is a run. Like if you hear thirty-two bulldog, that's a run play for you. Otherwise you're always the check-down."

"What's that?"

"It means you stay close to the line of scrimmage in case José needs to dump the ball off to someone."

"So I'm like his emergency exit?"

Aaron nodded. "Something like that. Anything hurt yet?" he asked, flipping a stick into the trees.

"Not really," I said, suddenly feeling disappointed for some weird reason. "I haven't even been tackled."

"You will be," Aaron replied. "But don't worry," he added. "The first hit is always the worst."

If that was Aaron's way of comforting me, it didn't

work. The fear of pain was the reason Spencer Randle scared me so much. With his size and strength, he could do some serious damage to me, and I liked being able to walk and breathe. Still, deep down, I wondered if Aaron was on to something. What if getting hit was the key to not being afraid of Spencer? Maybe Brian Braun marched around town like he owned the place because the fear had been knocked out of him. I wanted to know the answer more than anything; I just didn't want to pay the price.

●●●

Since it was too early for me to go home, I went to the drugstore to buy note cards. I sat on a bench in Boardman Park and wrote down the plays so I could memorize them before the next game. I figured it would be easy. After all, I'd memorized all the presidents, the state capitals, and the periodic table of elements in elementary school. Compared to that, this should have been a piece of cake.

Except when I went to the porch after dinner to study, I couldn't concentrate. It was too much pressure. If I forgot that Helena was the capital of Montana, nobody got smeared on the football field. Today it was José. Tomorrow it could be me. Spencer was still waiting for his chance to blow me up.

I found the football on the porch and walked backward ten paces. Gripping the football like Aaron had shown me, I aimed for the tire swing and let it fly. The football fluttered over the tire. Hoping nobody had seen that throw, I grabbed the football and tried again, getting closer. Again and again, I aimed for the tire swing, each time pretending to snap the ball to myself and retreating four steps like José always did before firing. After my tenth or twelfth attempt, my throws got straighter and faster, then closer to the tire swing. I felt my arm memorizing the motion like my brain had memorized prime numbers. Finally, I hit the bull's-eye, a beauty right through the tire.

"Hole in one!"

I turned around to see Evan standing at the gate. "How long have you been there?" I asked.

"Long enough to see you get one through," she said, sitting down on the grass.

Taking a seat not far away, I saw a splint on Evan's right ring finger. "What happened?"

"Jammed it in lacrosse," she said, examining her finger as she moved it slowly back and forth. "It's not broken, but Mom made me put this on anyway. We had it from the time I did break my finger."

"Are you ever afraid of getting hurt?"

"Oh, all the time," she said. "But that's just part of life. If I didn't want to get hurt, I'd have to stay inside all day doing nothing. No thanks. Or I guess I could play golf," she added, smiling.

"Ha, ha," I said.

"Sorry, couldn't resist."

"Don't worry about it," I said. "I'm not even . . ." I paused, unsure of whether to keep going. I wanted Evan to know that I was becoming a football player more than anything. So what was holding me back?

"I'm not going to golf camp," I told her.

"You're not?" Evan said. "What are you doing?"

"Flag football," I said. "At the rec center."

"I thought your parents wouldn't let you."

"They had a change of heart," I said, still wondering why I hadn't told Evan the whole truth. "I can be very convincing."

Evan plucked a dandelion and sent the seeds flying with a single breath. "So, are you afraid of getting hurt?" she asked.

The honest answer was yes, more than anything. But I had ditched golf camp to play in the League of Pain to prove I was tough enough for football. I couldn't admit now that I was scared. I had to be fearless, like Brian Braun. "Nope," I said. "No fear. That's my motto."

Evan lay on her back in the grass and stared up at the black and blue evening sky. "What do you think Dr. Pirate's motto is?"

I tried to think of a motto for Dr. Pirate, but I was too busy asking myself why I hadn't told Evan about the League of Pain. The League of Pain was the most secretive thing I had ever done, so why was it too secretive for Evan? I could only come up with one answer: I wasn't ready to tell Evan about the League of Pain because I wasn't really in it. Not yet, anyway. Not until I felt the pain.

CHAPTER NINETEEN

The fourth game between the Morons and the Idiots was a lot like the first. Knowing Spencer was waiting to lay me out, I did everything I could to avoid touching the football. I hid behind other receivers on pass plays and got out of the way whenever José handed the ball off to Aaron.

But the more I stayed out of trouble, the more scared I got about that first hit.

"I'm getting sick and tired of waiting," Spencer said to me as we passed each other before a kickoff. "If you don't get in the game for real, I'm going to bring the game to you. Got it?"

Part of me wanted to get in the game. Everyone

else had caught, run, or thrown the ball, and they all seemed like they were having a lot more fun than I was. This was Dad's fault, I told myself. If he had let me play flag football, I wouldn't be risking my life in the League of Pain.

Late in the second half, the Idiots were losing to the Morons by a touchdown. We were starting our last drive near midfield, which meant we didn't have far to go to score.

José yelled at us in the huddle. "We have to score on this drive. We *will* score on this drive!"

"They're doubling me on every play," said Aaron. "It's impossible to get open."

"Then beat the coverage," José shot back, "because I want to win. The losing is getting old, you got me?"

Planet nodded. "We got it, José."

"We'll score," Aaron promised.

"Let's go do it," José said. "Thirty-two eagle on two." He clapped loudly as we broke the huddle and stood behind Planet to call for the ball.

"Hut-hut!"

When Planet snapped the ball to José, Aaron and Ox began their routes. I moved toward the sideline but didn't go too far from José.

Spencer was almost through his ten-Mississippi count and Aaron was covered. Julian had dropped back into double coverage with Shane. In a moment of fear, I realized that meant I was wide open. "Nine Mississippi . . . ten Mississippi!" Spencer yelled. He charged forward, looking for a sack, but José dodged the tackle. Spencer was on his heels when José spotted me waiting in the flat.

I blinked. When I opened my eyes, José's throwing arm was fully extended and his hand was empty. A split second later, my eyes picked up the football spinning toward me on a tight spiral.

Images of catching the ball and running untouched into the end zone flashed through my mind as I lifted my hands. But then the image in my brain changed. Suddenly it wasn't me celebrating the game-winning score, it was Spencer standing over my scattered body parts. The fear was too strong. I pulled my hands down and let the football sail over my head.

Back near the line of scrimmage, José threw up his arms in disgust. I could see the other Idiots shaking their heads as they walked back to the huddle. "Terrible," I heard Planet mutter to Ox. "Even the kid with the busted ankle would be better than this guy."

I wasn't even sure I should join them. I wanted to be a football player so badly. But I was no Brian Braun. I was Quiet Wyatt, too afraid of getting tackled to even catch a ball.

That was when Aaron hit me.

He blindsided me, drilling me square in the ribs with his head and shoulders. The impact was so hard I could feel the air from my lungs slam into the back of my teeth as it rushed out of my chest. For a moment, I was hanging in midair as my feet left the ground and dangled over my head. One of my shoes left a grass stain on my nose as Aaron and I returned to earth simultaneously. I felt every rock and clump of dirt dig into my back while the weight of Aaron's body crushed me from the top.

Then it was over.

Aaron jumped up like nothing had happened.

I rolled over slowly. "What's the matter with you?" I yelled. "I'm on your team!"

"Are you hurt?" he asked.

I took a minute to check myself out. My lungs had filled with air again. I moved my extremities and limbs. Everything worked. "No," I said.

"Good. Then get up and get ready for the next play. It's only second down."

"Why'd you do that?" I asked, dusting off my shorts.

"You're not really in the game until you get hit," Aaron explained. "You got hit. Now you're in the game. Get it?"

"I think so," I said, starting to follow Aaron back to the huddle.

But Spencer stuck his palm on Aaron's chest.

"What's your problem?" Aaron asked, knocking Spencer's hand to the side.

"I wanted the first hit, Parker. He got me in trouble, not you."

"You're not gonna hit anyone," Aaron replied. "Wyatt didn't do anything to—"

Maybe it was the hit Aaron had laid on me, or maybe it was hearing him stand up for me. But something inside me wanted to end it with Spencer once and for all.

"You want to hit me?" I said, forcing my way in between Spencer and Aaron. "Here I am, Spencer. Hit me. Get your revenge."

There was no fear in me. I was one hundred percent ready for Spencer to slug me with every ounce of strength in his body. I knew I could handle it.

Spencer looked me up and down with the same old mad-dog scowl, but no hit came. He waved his hand like he was swatting away a bug. "Forget it," he said after a minute. "Let's just play football."

"Hey, Spencer," I said as he walked away.

Spencer looked over his shoulder. "What?"

"You owe me a dollar and twenty-five cents."

"I owe you what?"

"The day you left school for a corn dog, you took my money. I want it back, you flabby Moron."

Spencer was facing the other direction, so I couldn't see the expression on his face, but his shoulders were twitching like the Hulk about to bust out of his shirt. Only instead of rage, Spencer smirked and said, "I'll pay you later, you skinny Idiot."

For the first time in my life, I wasn't afraid of Spencer Randle. In fact, I wondered if I had gone too far by calling him a flabby Moron. Was it right for me to talk like that to Spencer just because he had talked that way to me? But I knew the difference right away. I would never, ever say what I just said to someone who couldn't fight back. That was what separated me from Spencer.

The Idiots won the game that day when Aaron intercepted a pass and ran it back for a touchdown. Even better, I finally left the field understanding why it was called the League of Pain. My side ached where Aaron had hit me and there was a gash on my knee from where I'd landed. It felt great.

I was walking past a pile of shirts and shoes when a football landed in the brush not far from me.

Someone behind me whistled. "Parker, little help?"

I turned around to see José pointing at the football. Not thinking much about it, I picked up the ball and tossed it back.

José caught the ball and tucked it under one arm. "Thanks!" he shouted.

Aaron appeared at my side. "Did you just throw that ball to José?" he asked.

"Yeah. Why?"

"Because that was like thirty yards and you were practically flat-footed."

"Is thirty yards good?"

"I guess your practice in the backyard is actually paying off."

"Maybe I should play quarterback," I said as a joke.

"Don't make me laugh," Aaron said.

We walked down the narrow path, passing through the deep shade of the forest. Somewhere nearby a woodpecker hammered into the bark of a pine tree, probably looking for lunch.

"I'm hungry," I said as we hopped over a log that had fallen across the trail. "Living a lie is tough."

"Tell me about it. But that's the price you pay for freedom. I mean, if you did what Mom and Dad wanted, you'd be up at the golf course right now listening to some doofus tell you how to hold a club."

"Yeah, but at least I'd get lunch."

"You want lunch?" Aaron asked me as we came out of the woods. "I'll get you lunch."

Aaron led me down the side streets and through a few alleys until we arrived at the back door of Corner Pizza. He knocked twice. A minute later, the door opened and his friend Will, wearing an apron covered with sauce stains, let us in. Will had a shaggy beard and thick earrings that had carved large holes in his earlobes.

Aaron and I followed Will into the empty restaurant. "We don't open until three, so you guys have the place to yourselves for a couple of hours." He handed Aaron a bucket of tokens. "Here, go crazy. I'll bring a pizza out in a minute."

"Thanks, man," Aaron said.

"How come he's doing this?" I asked. "Did you save his life or something?"

Aaron shook his head. "He's just doing it because he can. I mean, why not, right?"

"Yeah, but he could get in trouble."

"So could you, but you're here."

I couldn't deny that. I was eating pizza without paying for it after a football game my parents didn't know about when I should have been at the golf club with Francis. But I was only doing what I had seen Brian Braun and Aaron do, and nothing really bad ever seemed to happen to them. It made me wonder why they should get to have all the fun while everyone else had to follow the rules. It didn't seem fair. Besides, Will was *giving* us the pizza and the tokens. It's not like we were stealing them.

Plus, it was already working. Aaron was even treating me like a real person. If I had to break a few rules to make that happen, it was worth it to me.

It wasn't long before Will reappeared with a large

cheese pizza and two sodas. The three of us tore into our slices like piranhas.

"So you're still doing the football thing?" Will asked Aaron, brushing cheese from his chin.

"Me and him both are," Aaron replied.

"Really?" Will said with a look of surprise. "I mean, no offense, little man, but I can't picture you playing football."

"He plays bigger than he looks," Aaron said, before adding, "when he's not falling down on purpose in the middle of a play."

"Hey," I said. "I only did that once."

Aaron laughed. "Relax, Wyatt. I'm just giving you a hard time. If you're going to hang in the League of Pain you better get used to it."

"Yeah, man," Will said, nodding. "It's like, a sign of respect, right?"

"You could say that," Aaron said, reaching for another slice.

I savored every bite of that pizza. I was living the good life now. I was doing what I wanted to do and nobody could stop me. I was even eating lunch for free, with Aaron, who usually treated me like something caught in his teeth.

That afternoon, after I changed back into my golf clothes in the bathroom at the pizza place, I timed it so I got home five minutes after Dad and Kate—exactly how much longer it would take to bike from the golf course than drive. I'd thought of everything.

"Wyatt," said Dad, flipping through the mail. "How was golf camp today?"

"Great," I said, hopping off my bike. "I got a ball to the green with a six-iron."

Dad tossed a stack of envelopes and coupons into the recycle bin. "How are those shoes working out?"

"Not too bad."

Dad fixed his eyes on me. "I was looking for you when I picked up Kate. I saw Francis at the driving range but I didn't see you."

We were standing on the front stoop now.

"Who was he with?" I asked, hoping I sounded nice and casual.

"Young guy with blond hair and a red golf shirt. I figured he was your coach."

Shaking my head, I said, "Ah, nope. Our coach has dark hair and glasses. I don't know who that was."

"Where were you?" Dad asked, unlocking the door. He didn't sound suspicious, but I didn't know how long I could keep thinking on my feet.

"Bathroom," I said quickly. "Too much lemonade at lunch."

Laughing, Dad said, "If I keep missing you at the course, I'm going to start thinking you're off doing something else."

CHAPTER TWENTY

"See you later, Dad," I said on Friday morning, doing a quick lap around the driveway to get my bike in gear.

"Actually, I'll be out late tonight, pal," Dad said, sitting behind the wheel of his car. He started to roll up his window, then stopped. "Hey, why don't we play nine with Jim and Francis tomorrow?"

"Um, okay," I said, failing to come up with an excuse fast enough. "Sounds fun."

"Great," Dad said, giving me a thumbs-up. "I can't wait to see how you've improved."

"See you at golf camp!" Kate shouted from the backseat.

I showed up to the fifth game ready to play football. I wasn't afraid of Spencer Randle. I wasn't afraid of getting tackled. I just wanted to help the Idiots win.

Since José never gave me the ball on offense, I concentrated on defense. My job was to stick with Julian. But he was a rookie like me, so he didn't get a lot of action either.

Until game five.

About halfway through the game that day, Herc finally called a play for Julian.

Right before the snap I could tell something was up, because Julian kept looking over his shoulder at Herc. I took a step back so Julian couldn't get a jump on me. After the snap, Julian took off up the right sideline. I figured there was no way Herc would throw deep to a rookie, so when Julian made a move to the inside, I turned to follow him. Except Julian didn't actually go inside. He hit the accelerator and kept going. I'd bitten on the head fake and couldn't do anything but run after him. That was what I was doing when Herc hit him in stride for a long touchdown.

José put his arm around me after the play. "The next time he makes a move like that, jam him."

"Jam him?"

"Yeah, get in his way. Slow him down. Knock him off his route."

"Isn't that against the rules?"

"Man, this isn't the NFL. As long as you don't push a receiver down and sit on him, you can do whatever you want."

The next time we were on defense, I lined up across from Julian as usual. This was the same Julian I'd always been too scared to stand up to, even when he tied my shoes together or filled my batting helmet with dirt. Now I was about to jam him. It felt like revenge. "Ready to get burned, Parker?" Julian asked me.

"You couldn't burn me with a blowtorch," I said, playing farther off the line as Herc took the snap. Julian burst forward, ready to start his route, but I was already in motion and had the momentum. I didn't just jam him. I popped him with everything I had, shoulders first, right into the high part of his chest. Payback for years of treating me like I wasn't even a person.

Julian bounced backward and landed on the ground in a sitting position. He wasn't hurt, but a look of shock crossed his face.

"Are you crazy, Parker?" he said. "You can't hit me like that. I don't even have the ball."

"You're not gonna get the ball either if you keep falling down."

Julian stood up and got in my face. He was still three inches taller than me, but I didn't back away. "So that's how it is now?" he said.

Some of the other players were gathered around me and Julian, ready for one of us to take the first swing. I said, "This is the League of Pain, not the League of Please Don't Hit Me. If you don't like it, find another sport."

I heard a few oohs from the other guys. I had never heard anyone say *ooh* about anything I said.

"I know what it's called," Julian replied after a moment. "I'm not stupid."

"No, you're a Moron."

A few people laughed. Julian blinked, looking almost embarrassed. *Good,* I thought. Now he would know how it felt to be put down in front of other people. I wasn't about to go into the bully business myself, but if giving Julian a hard time made him think twice about doing it to someone else, it was worth it.

Herc didn't throw to Julian for the rest of that possession. The Morons ended up punting and we got the ball back deep in our own territory.

"Get ready," Julian said, glancing across the line of scrimmage. "What goes around comes around."

José called out the play as my toes danced in my shoes. I was about to get so open he'd have to throw to me. All because Julian wanted to hit me.

When the play started, Julian and I ran straight toward each other. But at the moment I expected him to hit me, I dropped to the ground and rolled right underneath him. When I popped back to my feet, Julian was six steps behind me. I waved my arms at José. Without hesitating, he fired the ball to me as I crossed the field from right to left. I caught the pass in stride and turned upfield. By that time the rest of the defense knew I had the football and they came after me like a swarm of bees. I thought about getting out of bounds to avoid the contact, but up ahead, I could see the end zone. It was so close, I had to go for it. So I turned back inside, barely slowing down. The defense had been coming so fast, they couldn't change directions. The only thing between me and the end zone was twenty yards of dirt and rocks. I crossed the goal line and dropped the football. It was my first touchdown in the League of Pain.

I hope it won't be my last, I thought as I took my time heading down the trail that led away from the field.

"Hey, Parker!" I heard someone yell while I was riding my bike slowly through the part of the park that was mostly thick forest.

After stopping to turn and look, I saw Spencer Randle huffing and puffing up the path. I almost laughed thinking that a month ago the sight of Spencer coming up behind me in the middle of a dark forest would have been my worst nightmare. Now I was actually glad to have somebody to walk with.

"What's up," I said, hopping off my bike.

"Sweet touchdown today," Spencer replied between heavy breaths. "I didn't know you could move like that."

"I've had a lot of practice running away from people who are bigger than me."

Spencer looked at me like he was going to respond, but he just nodded and frowned. I had a feeling that was as close as I would ever get to an apology from him.

We walked together until we got to the park entrance, where we split and went our own ways. I rode off alone, wondering if that was Spencer in a rare friendly mood, or if that was Spencer trying to be my friend.

After dinner, I told Evan all about my touchdown.

"Stand there," I said, pointing to a spot about ten feet away from me. "That's where Julian was. When I start running, come toward me."

"Got it," Evan said.

We acted it out in slow motion. I showed her how

I made Julian miss me. "Then I was wide open. I mean wiiiiide open. José, he's the QB, hit me and I just went . . . *boom* . . . supersonic. The next thing I knew I was in the end zone."

"Your talent would be wasted on the golf course," she said. "Imagine if your parents had made you do that. I mean, nothing against golf, but this is way cooler."

Evan gave me a high five. We held hands in midair. It wasn't like holding hands in a movie theater, but it was close, and I liked it. I wondered if she did too.

"You want to know what happened at the pool today?" she said after we had unlocked hands.

"What?" In all the excitement, I'd forgotten about Evan's job at the pool. With Brian Braun.

"Well, there's a good thing and a bad thing. Which one do you want to hear first?"

"The good thing," I said, sitting down on the grass to listen to Evan's news.

"I saved someone's life!" she shouted.

"Get out of here."

"Okay, to be honest, I can't say for one hundred percent sure he would have died, but if I hadn't seen the kid sinking and told the lifeguard, and if the lifeguard hadn't jumped in the pool, that kid could have gone to the bottom."

"With the fishes," I said.

159

"With the fishes," Evan replied.

"Did you get a medal or anything?"

"I'm not in it for the glory, Wyatt," she said with a smile. "I was just doing my job. Aren't you proud of me?"

I was proud of Evan. She was the coolest person I knew. "I'm bursting with pride," I told her. "You're an American hero."

"Probably," Evan said.

"So what's the bad thing?"

Evan shook her head slowly. "I don't want to say. It's too sad."

"Sadder than someone almost drowning?"

"Sadder than someone actually drowning."

I looked at Evan. "What, does Brian Braun have a girlfriend or something?"

Her eyes seemed to pop out of her head. "Who told you that?"

"Who told me what?"

"That Brian has a girlfriend!"

"Wait, I was right? I was just kidding."

Evan toppled to the ground and lay flat on her back. "Well, it's not funny. I'm totally wrecked. You should have seen them sharing a milk shake at the snack stand. He didn't even pay for it."

Man, did that guy pay for anything? I couldn't decide if Brian Braun was my rival or my hero.

"Why are you smiling?" Evan asked me.

160

"I'm not smiling."

"Yes you are. I can see your teeth. What's up? I'm dying of a broken heart here and you're enjoying it. I thought you were my friend."

"Maybe I think the good thing is more good than the bad thing is bad."

Evan propped herself up on her elbows. "You might be right. I saved someone's life. That's a way bigger deal. Starting tomorrow, I'm over Brian."

I liked the sound of that.

Neither of us said anything for a while. Eventually, Evan sighed, rising to her feet, and said good night. I stood up too, feeling the aches in my side and legs. Looking at my body more closely, I saw a bruise on my calf and a few small cuts on my knees. It all came with a little bit of pain, but it was definitely worth it.

Mom was looking for me when I came into the kitchen, blinking from the bright light. "Phone for you, Wyatt," she said. "It's Francis."

I wished I could tell Mom to take a message, but that would raise too many questions. I knew I had to take the call, even though I didn't really have anything to say. Francis thought I was lying low this summer, so I couldn't tell him about football. He'd never get it.

"Okay," I said, taking the phone from her. "Francis, what's up?"

"Five words," said Francis. *"I. E. Two. Three. D."*

"You what too?"

"No," Francis corrected me before repeating himself, more slowly this time. "*I . . . E . . . Two . . . Three . . . D. Invasion Earth Two* in three-D!"

"Oh yeah. I know. It's out now. What about it?"

"We're going tomorrow."

"Who is?"

"Us. Me and you. After golf."

Francis did a lot of things that bugged me. Telling me that I was going to do something with him instead of asking me might have been at the top of the list. It wasn't cool when my parents did it and it definitely wasn't cool when he did it. Still, I knew I had to keep him happy since he was keeping a big secret for me.

"Sure," I told him. "I'm in."

"Sweet," Francis said. "Golf and a movie. Could be the perfect day."

CHAPTER TWENTY-ONE

Gripping a golf club with sweaty hands was not easy, but I couldn't calm my nerves. Not while Francis was standing five feet away chatting with my dad. One wrong word from him and my life as I knew it would be finished. I tried to focus on the ball at my feet, but I couldn't help listening.

"So, Alan," I heard Francis ask Dad. "How's your portfolio looking?"

Jim was off in the woods, looking for a ball he'd shanked off the tee.

"Not bad, Francis," said Dad, like it was totally normal for one of my friends to ask him about his portfolio. "Market's been up, so that's good for everyone. Why do you ask?"

"Oh, no reason," said Francis, leaning on his club. "I was just thinking if you needed any ideas I'd tell you about this new company that's about to go public. Normally, I wouldn't advise taking a big position on one stock, but it might be the perfect move. In your case, I mean."

The club almost slipped out of my hand. What was Francis doing? Why couldn't he keep his mouth shut like he promised? And how had I ended up being friends with the only fourteen-year-old on the planet who paid attention to the stock market?

"In my case?" Dad asked. "What do you mean?"

Francis seemed to realize his mistake and started backpedaling. "Oh, I mean, just because you're kind of a gambler."

"I don't know about that," said Dad, losing interest in the conversation. "Hey, Wyatt," he called. "Let 'er rip. There's a group behind us."

Doing my best to swing without letting the club fly out of my hands, I hacked at the ball, knocking it a hundred yards straight as an arrow.

"Good enough," said Dad.

We shouldered our bags and started hiking up the fairway. Dad veered toward me. "Everything okay?" he asked. "You seem a little distracted."

"Nothing's wrong," I said. "Just thirsty."

"Well, it's great being out here with you," he said,

putting his arm around me. "You're turning into a real golfer."

"I am?"

Dad laughed. "Yeah, you're on the second hole and you're already thinking about the clubhouse."

• • •

That afternoon Francis and I went to see *Invasion Earth 2 3D*.

"Two for *I E Two Three-D*," Francis said.

"Two?" I asked as Francis paid for the tickets.

"Yeah," he said. "It's on me. I won a few bets with my dad on the course this morning."

"Oh, okay. Thanks. That's really cool."

"No problem," Francis said. "Just don't try to hold my hand or anything."

"You need to get over yourself," I said as we waited in the lobby. "You're not even my type."

That made Francis crack up.

We were still standing around waiting for our theater to start seating people when Francis turned white. "Oh no," he said.

I felt a thick arm wrap around my neck. The headlock lasted only a second before I was free. I heard a familiar laugh behind me and turned around to see Spencer Randle, Planet, and Ox.

"Guess who?" said Spencer.

"Looks like two Idiots and a Moron to me," I said.

"Idiots rule," said Planet.

"Then why are we winning?" Spencer asked.

Planet poked his finger at Spencer. "It's not because of you."

"Shut up," said Spencer. "I'll drop you right here like I did yesterday."

"You mean right before I tackled you?" I asked.

Ox and Planet lost it, which made Spencer shove them both at the same time. All three guys stumbled into a display for a movie called *Will You Be My Dragon?*

I looked over at Francis, who was hanging back, gripping his ticket in his hands. "Relax," I told him. "They're cool."

"Um, that's Spencer *Randle*," Francis said. "The guy who wanted to destroy you."

"Okay, look," I said, pulling Francis aside. "There's something I haven't told you. I've kind of been playing football this summer."

"Where?" Francis asked. "With who?"

"In the park," I replied, starting to feel like I was talking to my mom. "With Spencer and some other guys."

"*Why?*" Francis asked.

"Because I want to. Because it's fun and I'm actually pretty good at it." A few feet away, Ox body-slammed Planet into the wall. "But you can't tell anybody."

"There's a lot about you I can't tell anyone," Francis said, sounding annoyed and suspicious at the same time.

"Please don't make a big deal out of it, Francis. It's just football. It's not like we're robbing banks."

"Okay," said Francis. "I won't tell anyone you're playing the world's dumbest sport with the world's biggest boneheads."

That was all I wanted to hear. I didn't need Francis's approval. I just had to know he wouldn't talk.

Planet, Ox, and Spencer finished wrestling. Planet looked up at the big screen. "Oh man, *Octosaur* starts in two minutes. We better go now. I want a good seat. In the middle."

Spencer pointed at Planet's gut. "Don't you mean you want two seats?" he said.

"Keep talking and I'll make you my seat," Planet shot back. "And I had a burrito for breakfast."

"All right, all right," Spencer said. "Let's go in." He looked at me. "You coming?"

"We're seeing *I E Two Three-D*," Francis said.

"You're seeing what?" Ox asked. "I pee on you?"

"*Invasion Earth Two Three-D*," I said. "It's about aliens, and they—"

Spencer cut me off. "*Octosaur* is better. I'm talking about a T. rex with eight legs that can shoot ink out of his butt. It's the most awesome thing that ever lived."

"You have to admit, it does sound pretty awesome," I said to Francis.

"I thought we were seeing *Invasion Earth*," Francis said. "Besides, *Octosaur* is rated R. We could get in trouble."

I looked over at the entrance to the theaters. Planet and Spencer had run ahead to get good seats. Ox waved at me and Francis. "Hey, ladies, are you coming or not?"

"They don't even check what movie you're going to," I said, getting impatient. I didn't understand why Francis had to be so stubborn. It wasn't like *Invasion Earth* was showing for only one day. "They just care if you have a ticket."

"You can see *Octosaur* if you want," Francis snapped. "I bought a ticket to *Invasion Earth* and that's what I'm seeing."

I watched Francis march away, but I didn't follow him. I had better things to do than sit next to someone who had to have it his way all the time.

"Wait up," I called to Ox. "I'm coming."

Octosaur must have been longer than *Invasion Earth,* because there was no sign of Francis when

I came out of the theater. I felt a little guilty about not seeing the movie with him, especially since he'd paid for my ticket. But I did what I'd wanted to do. Being in the League of Pain was about more than just showing up to play football. It was also about being a part of the group. Francis couldn't see that because he never took any chances or tried to make new friends. If he did, he'd understand why I went to see *Octosaur* instead of *IE23D*. Also, I bet if it had been the other way around and Francis had changed his mind, he would have expected me to follow him.

After the movie, I went with Planet and Ox to Pilchuck Market, where I bought a bag of potato chips. Spencer had left the theater on his own, saying he had something to take care of. I smiled, remembering when I had been the something he had to take care of. Now here I was hanging out with two guys who were even bigger than Spencer.

Planet was standing in the candy aisle, begging Ox to buy him a candy bar.

"Buy your own," said Ox. "I only have enough for one."

"I would buy my own, but I spent my money paying for your extra-large soda, *remember*?"

"Fine," said Ox, looking around the store. "You want a candy bar, I'll get you a candy bar."

Then, right before my eyes, Ox grabbed two candy

bars from the rack and casually slipped one into his pocket before taking the second candy bar to the counter. It all happened in a split second. The next thing I knew, we were back outside the store.

At first I couldn't believe what I'd seen. I had never watched anybody steal right in front of my eyes. For a moment, I was tempted to tell Planet and Ox that shoplifting wasn't my idea of a good time. But that seemed exactly like something Francis would do. So I decided not to judge them before I got to know them.

"How'd you know you wouldn't get caught?" I asked Ox.

Ox took the candy bar from his pocket and tossed it to Planet. He pointed at the clerk back inside the store. "Once he sees you're buying something, he doesn't pay attention to anything else you're doing," he explained. "He's too excited to get his hands on the money."

Planet ripped off a chunk of the candy bar with his teeth. "His fault for being so greedy." He started laughing as bits of chocolate flew from his mouth and landed on Ox's shirt.

That made me and Planet laugh too. It felt a bit funny to be laughing right after watching someone commit a crime, but I figured Ox had a point. What was the big deal about one candy bar? After all, if it was cool for Brian Braun to get into a movie without paying, why shouldn't it be cool to get a snack without paying?

"So you're in eighth grade?" Ox asked when we had all calmed down.

"I was in eighth grade. I'll be in ninth grade when school starts. What grade are you in?"

"We're both in tenth grade," Planet answered.

"Do you like high school?"

"Definitely," said Ox. "It kicks middle school's butt. There's a lot more people to hang out with, for one thing."

"And you can go off campus for lunch," Planet added.

Spencer would like that, I thought.

We hung around Pilchuck Market for a long time while Planet and Ox told me all about high school. They even promised to make sure nobody gave me a hard time. "Idiots have to look out for Idiots," Ox said.

• • •

Later that night, I was in my room wearing a pair of shorts when Mom cruised by carrying a basket of laundry. "Anything to wash?" she asked, poking her head in the doorway.

"Just these," I said, tossing Mom the mostly clean golf clothes I had been changing in and out of like Superman. Only instead of using a phone booth, I'd been hiding behind large trees.

Squinting, Mom took a few steps toward me. "Wyatt," she said, "what's that bruise on your thigh? Did you get that playing golf?"

"What bruise?"

"Honey, I'm your mother and a nurse. You can't walk in this house with a bruise without me noticing. Now tell me how that happened."

"I got hit by a cart," I said.

"You got hit by a cart?"

"Well, I mean, I hit the cart. I wasn't watching where I was going and I walked right into it."

"You must have been walking pretty fast," said Mom, examining the bruise more closely.

"Mom, stop looking at my leg," I said, pulling my shorts down so they covered my thigh. "It's fine. It's just a bruise."

"Maybe you should ice it," she said.

"If it was going to swell, it would be swollen already. You should know that," I said.

"You're right," Mom said, smiling. "I guess it's hard to be a mother and a nurse at the same time. I'll leave you alone. But if it starts to hurt, let me know. We've got some ibuprofen in the bathroom."

"Deal," I said, escorting her to my door.

At first, I was pleased with myself for wriggling out of another jam, but as I tried to fall asleep, I felt more and more restless. Up until that night, I had been sleeping soundly. Tackle football on a rocky field with guys twice my size trying to bury me was enough to wear me out. Now the ache wasn't in my thigh, my hand, or my ribs. It was in my head. Every time I pictured Mom, Dad, Francis, or whoever else I had deceived, my brain throbbed just a little bit. And there were still ten days left until the Fourth of July.

CHAPTER TWENTY-TWO

"Will you pass the butter?" I asked Kate on Wednesday morning.

We were wolfing down breakfast before Dad came downstairs to drive her to the golf course.

Handing over the butter, Kate asked in a whisper, "Are you getting excited?"

"About the butter?"

"No!" she said, shaking her head rapidly. "About the Fourth of July. Remember, your date with Evan?"

"It's not a date," I said. "It's just a bunch of people sitting on a hill watching fireworks."

"Like who?" she asked.

"Like people you don't know who work at the pool with Evan."

"You mean Brian and Ashley?"

"How do you know about Brian?"

"My friend Caitlin from golf is Ashley's sister, which makes me and Brian practically related," Kate explained as she took a glass from the cupboard. "Plus, duh, everyone knows Brian Braun is the best football player ever from Pilchuck."

She paused to pour herself a glass of juice. "Anyway, Caitlin told me Brian lives next door to them and he and Ashley have been friends forever. Now they'll probably never break up. But if they do, one of them will probably have to move because it'll be totally awkward."

I took all this in and decided that it was definitely good news. Brian was out of the way, and if Evan was looking for another football player to be the man of her dreams, all she had to do was walk next door. So what if I had to put up with a little guilt now and then? It was worth it.

Dad came into the kitchen just as Kate and I were finishing. "Ready, pumpkin?" he asked her.

"Ready, squash," said Kate, following Dad to the front door.

"You sure you don't want a ride?" Dad asked me a minute later in the driveway, where Aaron and I were getting on our bikes.

"I'm sure," I said.

"Okay," he replied. "But I'll see you at the golf course at four o'clock."

"You will?"

"That's when camp ends, right?"

"Ah, yep."

"Well, the golf tournament is only a week away and I need to practice. I thought we could play a few holes together. Maybe you can give me some pointers."

I froze. I couldn't think fast enough. My mind was jammed up.

"Is something wrong?" Dad asked.

"He's just too excited to speak," Aaron said.

Dad looked me in the eye. "Is that it, Wyatt?"

I managed to nod. "I'll be there," I said.

"Great," Dad said as he got into his car. "I'll see you this afternoon. Meet me by the first hole."

"Block it out," Aaron said after Dad had driven away. "There's nothing you can do about it now, so forget about it and think football. We need to beat the Morons today."

I did my best to put golf out of my mind. I figured I'd have plenty of time to make it to the golf course by four o'clock.

• • •

As soon as the game started, football was the only thing in the world. All I had to do was get open and wait for José to hit me, just like he'd done last Friday.

Except it wasn't that easy.

"Do you know what this is?" Julian asked the first time we had the ball. He curled his fingers and thumb together to make a zero with his right hand.

"The size of your brain?" I said.

"This is how many times you're going to catch the ball today."

"Just try and stop me."

That was just what Julian did. He stuck to me like superglue. It wasn't too difficult, since José didn't call any plays for me.

When he did, Spencer always watched me out of the corner of his eye while he did his ten-Mississippi count.

We had a chance to win the game, but our final drive stalled at midfield when we couldn't get two completions.

After the game, I overheard my teammates complaining. "We can't move the ball unless everyone on the team is a threat," I heard Ox say to José.

I knew he was talking about me.

"I know," José said. "I'll come up with something for tomorrow."

"At least we're playing good D," said Aaron.

That started a conversation about defense. I would

have stayed to listen, but I had to get up to the golf course so I could practice before meeting Dad.

• • •

It was a little after three when I locked my bike in front of the main entrance to the Pilchuck Golf and Tennis Club. Golfers in carts rolled past me on their way to the first tee, while other people sat on the deck soaking up the sunshine. Besides the sound of balls being smacked on the driving range, it was as quiet as a library. Maybe a nice place to visit, I thought, walking to the clubhouse to check out golf clubs, but I needed more noise and action.

Inside the clubhouse, I went to the counter, where a lady in a plaid sweater was folding shirts. Her name tag said Jo.

It was the woman I'd spoken to on the phone the day I called to say I wasn't coming to golf camp.

"Can I help you?" she asked, eyeing me suspiciously, like I didn't belong.

"Yeah, um, can I go to the driving range?"

"You need to be a member," Jo explained sternly. "Are you a member?"

"My dad is. His name is Alan Parker."

As soon as I mentioned Dad's name, Jo gave me a wide smile. "Are you Wyatt?"

I was glad to see Jo was warming up to me, but I hoped she and Dad weren't too tight. What if she asked him about space camp? I decided to answer cautiously. "Uh-huh."

"It's nice to meet you, Wyatt," Jo said. "How is your dad? He hasn't been around much lately."

"He's been busy with work."

"And tell me, how is space camp?"

"Space camp is, um, out of this world," I said, figuring a little humor would keep Jo from asking too many questions.

Jo thought that was hilarious. "The driving range is right through there," she said, pointing out the glass door. "You can borrow a club. Just take a bucket of balls and choose any tee you want."

I found a tee far away from everyone else and set up a ball. I gripped the three-wood like Dad had showed me. Bringing the club back, I drove it forward, swiveling my hips as I swung—right over the ball. I tried again and the head of the club bumped the ball off the tee.

By the time the bucket was empty, I was getting them in the air. I wasn't hitting anything two hundred yards like Francis, but it would be good enough to impress Dad.

I had hit about half the balls in my second bucket

when Dad arrived. "Jo told me I'd find you here," he said.

"Did she say anything else?" I asked.

Dad gave me a funny look. "Well, she did ask me if you were enjoying space camp. Any idea what that was about?"

"Space camp?" I said.

Dad took the cover off his driver. "That's what I thought. But maybe I misunderstood. It was pretty busy in there and Jo can be a little, you know." Dad twirled a finger by his ear.

"What did you tell her?"

Dad punched me softly in the shoulder. "I told her you were having a blast."

"Good one."

He winked at me. "I thought so."

It felt good hanging out with Dad. Playing golf wasn't too bad either. The more I hit, the better I got. And the better I got, the more fun I had. After a while, we decided to play a few holes. I didn't come close to par, but at least I didn't have to pick up my ball.

We ended the day drinking lemonades on the deck. "You know what I see?" Dad asked. "I see someone playing with a lot more confidence."

"Me?"

"You bet," Dad said. "It's not just here either. I've noticed it at home too. You're growing up, Wyatt."

"You got all that from a round of golf?"

"Smart alec. I'm trying to give you a compliment." Dad signed for the bill and we got ready to leave. "And listen, if you decide in the end that golf isn't your thing, I'll respect that and you can try any sport you want."

I hope that includes football, I thought, imagining how nice it would be to play a game without having to lead a secret life.

CHAPTER TWENTY-THREE

José drew up a trick play in the huddle. "We're gonna run a flea-flicker," he said. "You know how that works? I hand off to you"—he pointed to Aaron—"and you pitch it back to me. If the Morons bite on the run, someone should be open for a long pass."

José started the play with a hand-off to Aaron, who took a few steps forward and pitched the ball back. José pumped his right arm, looking for an open receiver.

When Spencer got to ten Mississippi, José scrambled upfield, but the defense closed in and tackled him quickly.

It was second down.

"Okay, that didn't work," José said before the next play. "This time line up like usual. Receivers on the ends and backs behind me. Aaron, when I snap it, you follow my lead. I'm going to hand it to you." José drew a diagram in the dirt. "When you get back to the line of scrimmage, you either hit someone downfield or keep running."

José put the play in motion, but Aaron bobbled the hand-off. He didn't fumble, but he had to slow down. By the time he turned the corner, the Morons were ready. They forced him out of bounds for no gain.

Third down.

José stayed cool, but I knew he was starting to sweat inside. We still had a chance to win the game, but if we lost, the season would practically be over.

"Forget the tricks," he said. "Thirty-three falcon on two." He looked at Aaron. "You line up in the slot, like a tight end."

Turning to me, he said, "You're the back on this one. Get ready, just in case."

We got into position. Planet held the football in his hands and waited for José to call for the snap from the shotgun.

Suddenly José stood up straight. "Stampede, stampede!" he yelled just as Planet hiked the ball, sending it right into my hands. Just like that, I was the quarterback.

Seeing what had happened, José became a blocker. He, Ox, and Planet stood between me and the rushing Morons.

I knew I could either throw the ball or run it. I moved sideways across the field, trying to get a clear look at the receivers. I saw Aaron get open for a second, just as Spencer closed in on me. I raised my arm to throw the ball as Spencer jumped into the air, but I scooted by him. Bodies flew at me, but I dodged them, freezing Herc with a stutter step and spinning around Julian. I raced down the sideline toward the boulders. I was ten yards from the end zone when Julian hit me in the side like he was fired from a cannon. I landed ten feet out of bounds and skidded across a bed of tiny rocks.

I could feel the blood flowing out of my hands, arms, and legs, but it didn't bother me. I jumped right up and carried the football back to the huddle.

"I got one word for you," said José, putting his arm around me. "*Wildcat.*"

"What does that mean?" I asked.

"You're gonna take the snap from Planet. I'm going to line up as an extra lineman. Aaron is your receiver. If he's open, hit him. If he's not, run it yourself."

"I don't know about this," said Planet. "How do we even know he can throw?"

"He can throw," said José. "Just do your job so Wyatt can do his."

As we broke out of the huddle, I looked at the other team and saw five guys who were all bigger than me, but there was just one thought in my head: *You might knock me over, but you are not going to keep me down.* It was the same feeling that had hit me like a bolt of lightning in my baseball game and sent me charging into the catcher. Only this time, the feeling lasted a lot longer than a few seconds. For the rest of the game, snap after snap, drive after drive, I played football fearlessly. I got hit, clocked, smacked, and dropped, but I kept running, throwing, ducking. Whatever I had to do to move the ball closer to the end zone, I did.

And when I scored the winning touchdown on a sweep up the right sideline, the Idiots mobbed me the same way my baseball team had. I knew I was one of them—an Idiot and a football player.

CHAPTER TWENTY-FOUR

On Saturday Evan and I had plans to see *Dr. Pirate*. My pulse was racing as I walked to the pool to meet her. It was the last weekend before the Fourth of July and things were getting hot. Today we were going to the movies and soon I'd be watching the fireworks with Evan on the hill, where who knows what could happen. But the more I thought about that, the more aware I was of how quickly it could all end. One slipup and Mom and Dad would bust me. I had to keep thinking like Aaron or Brian—be ready for anything and show no fear.

When I got to the pool, Brian Braun was there with his dumb muscles ready to save someone from drowning, but Evan hardly looked at him.

"So where's Ashley?" I asked, taking a seat at the picnic bench outside the snack bar, where we had ordered ice cream.

Evan sat across from me, wearing shorts over a red bathing suit and brown sunglasses that covered half her face. "Get this," she said, removing the sunglasses since we were under the shade of an umbrella. "She dumped him."

"She did?"

"Like third-period French."

"What happened?"

"I don't know the details," Evan replied. "But I'm going to find out."

"Are you still, you know, over him?" I asked.

"Eh," said Evan, unwrapping her ice cream bar. "I was never really that into him."

"If you say so." I decided not to remind her about the time she picked trash out of a garbage can just so she'd have an excuse to stand near him.

"You're still coming to watch the fireworks, right?" Evan asked, kicking me under the table.

I thought I was seeing fireworks already. But I did my best to stay cool. "Definitely," I said, taking small sips of my milk shake to make the moment last as long as possible.

"Wanna hear a joke?" I asked as we walked through town on the way to the movies.

"Is it funny?"

"No," I said.

"I still want to hear it."

"Where does Dr. Pirate work?"

Evan answered immediately. "I give up."

"The E *arrrgh*."

"That is the worst joke I have heard in my entire life," Evan said.

"Thank you." I knew it was lame, but telling bad jokes eased my mind.

We went another block. "I'm glad I'm seeing this movie with you," Evan said. "I told my friends on the lacrosse team I thought it looked good and they laughed at me."

"You've had a tough week," I said.

"Tell me about it," Evan replied. "What did your friends say when you told them you wanted to see *Dr. Pirate*?"

I wasn't sure how to answer that. At the moment, I wasn't even sure who my friends were. Except Evan. There was no doubt about Evan. "It didn't really come up," I answered after a second.

A few minutes later we were standing in front of Pilchuck Market. "Let's go in," said Evan, reaching for the door. "I want some Milk Duds. Actually, I want some Red Vines." She let go of the door. "Oh man, I want both."

"So get both," I said.

Evan sighed. "I only have enough for one."

"Don't worry about that," I said. "You can have both."

"What do you mean?"

"You want snacks? I'll get you snacks."

"That's so sweet," Evan said. "I'll totally pay you back."

I scoped out the store as we made our way to the candy aisle. Up at the counter, the same clerk who was working when I came with Planet and Ox was busy helping an old lady who wanted her food bagged carefully.

My mind was clear as I found the Red Vines and handed them to Evan. I knew what I was about to do was wrong, but I was afraid to chicken out. Like by going through with it, I'd be proving to myself that I could make it through the whole season in the League of Pain without getting caught. I was giving myself a test I had to pass.

I picked out a bag of M&M's for myself. Then I grabbed a box of Milk Duds. I glanced quickly at the counter, then started to slip the Milk Duds into my pocket, imagining I was Brian Braun walking into the movie theater.

Evan grabbed my wrist. "Wyatt! Are you crazy? What are you doing?"

"You said you wanted Milk Duds."

"Not like *that*."

Evan locked her eyes on me. There was no escaping her glare. I blinked, then felt my hands begin to tremble. I dropped the Milk Duds back onto the rack. I didn't understand why I was shaking. The clerk hadn't even noticed. I still felt like a criminal. And not just because I had almost stolen a box of candy.

"What's wrong with you?" Evan asked.

Before I could answer her, the clerk walked up to us. "Finding everything okay?" he asked.

I instantly raised both my hands, showing him the bag of M&M's. Evan held up the Red Vines.

"All right," said the clerk. "Why don't you come with me and I'll ring you up?"

We paid for the candy and left the store.

"What's wrong with you?" Evan asked again.

"Nothing," I said. "Just forget it. It was a stupid idea." But it wasn't nothing, and I knew it.

"Just forget it?" Evan shot back. "You just tried to steal, Wyatt. You could have gotten us both in big trouble. How am I supposed to forget that?"

"But I didn't, did I?" Of course we both knew that if Evan hadn't stopped me, I would have stolen the candy. Realizing that made me feel queasy, even though I was living the life I had wanted, doing what I wanted to do, taking what I wanted, like Brian

Braun in the movie theater. Brian had made it look so easy, just like Ox had. Obviously there were some big differences between them and me. For the first time all summer, I was really scared. Not scared of getting tackled, but scared of being someone I didn't want to be. I could feel my conscience starting to break apart.

Evan and I made our way in awkward silence toward the movie theater. There was a bug in my gut, like the first moment of the flu, and even in the warm summer sun, I felt a chill.

"Are you okay?" Evan asked as we approached the theater a few blocks later. "You look pale."

"I'm fine," I said, forcing a smile. "Let's get our tickets."

I barely paid attention to *Dr. Pirate*. It might have been hilarious, or it might have been the stupidest movie ever made. I wasn't sure because I couldn't stop thinking about what had happened in Pilchuck Market. I wasn't going to forget the way Evan had looked at me in the candy aisle. It made me wonder how Mom and Dad or Francis would look at me if they found out what I'd done to them. Maybe the only thing worse would be how I'd look at myself.

CHAPTER TWENTY-FIVE

I didn't realize how strong José was until the end of our game on Tuesday, when he lifted me off the ground, celebrating my game-winning touchdown, off a bootleg that had fooled the Morons so badly, I'd high-stepped in untouched from ten yards out.

"That was ferocious, Parker!" José shouted.

The next thing I knew, I was back on the ground, standing in a circle with the other Idiots, our arms locked as we swayed.

"We are . . . ," José yelled.

"Idiots!" we screamed back.

"We are . . ."

"Idiots!"

We had never celebrated a win like this, but then again, this was no ordinary win. We had tied the season score at six games each, which meant that tomorrow's game would be for the championship.

I was still fired up that evening, already day-dreaming about winning the big game on the Fourth of July, then heading up the hill to watch the fireworks with Evan. I felt like the luckiest guy on earth.

Unfortunately, my luck was about to run out. It started with Aaron pulling me and Kate into my room.

"I think they're getting suspicious," Aaron said. We were in the same spot where we had taken our oath just a few weeks earlier.

"This is just like *Don't Tell Mom I'm a Mermaid*," Kate said, nodding.

"What do you mean?" I said. "What happened?"

"Well, the mermaid's parents found all these shells in her bedroom and—"

"Not to the mermaid!" I snapped. "I mean, what happened with Mom and Dad. Why are they suspicious?"

"Not sure," Aaron answered, looking unusually nervous. "All I know is Mom and Dad want to talk to both of us in the kitchen before dinner."

"What do we do?" I asked, suddenly terrified I was about to be crushed by the full weight of my lies.

"First, we're not going to panic," Aaron said. "Just

follow my lead. If we play it right, we can limit the damage."

"What's that supposed to mean?"

"If one of us takes the fall," said Aaron, "it'll take the heat off me."

"Oh, that's nice," I said. "Sacrifice me."

"Or her," Aaron said, pointing at Kate.

"That is not how the mermaid oath goes," she shot back. "The oath says *We mermaids three under sky and in the sea—*"

"Kate," Aaron growled. "I swear, if you say one more word about mermaids, I will throw you into the ocean myself."

"Sorry!" Kate cried. "I won't say anything else about mermaids. If you want to make Mom and Dad mad at me, that's fine. I'll get in less trouble than you anyway. Just don't kick me out of the group."

"What group?" I said.

Kate pointed at me and Aaron, then herself. "Us," she said.

"We're not a group," I said, figuring I'd say it before Aaron did.

"Then why are we all hanging out in your room?" Kate asked. "We never used to do that." She hung her head and muttered, "Until the oath."

• • •

Suddenly, we heard Mom's voice calling from the kitchen. "Wyatt and Aaron, come down here, please."

Aaron and I looked at each other.

"You ready?" he asked me.

"I guess so."

"Seriously, man, it's going to be all right. And whatever happens, we're in this together."

"Thanks," I said, sensing that Aaron actually meant it. Trusting him to look out for me, I took a deep breath and tried to relax.

"Let's get this over with," he said, leading the way to the stairs.

Kate came running after us. "Can I come?" she asked, peering over the railing.

"You're better off staying up there," Aaron answered. "But we'll hang out again. And I promise, we won't tell Mom you're a mermaid."

CHAPTER TWENTY-SIX

"Have a seat," Mom said, waving to the two empty chairs at the kitchen table, where she and Dad sat facing each other.

"What's going on?" Aaron asked, doing his best to sound casual.

"We'd like to know if you were at Corner Pizza last Wednesday afternoon."

Aaron and I made eye contact for a millisecond. For me, it was long enough to decide that if Mom and Dad knew enough to ask, denying the truth would be pointless.

"Okay, you got us," Aaron said. "We were downtown and I had to use the bathroom. My friend Will works there and he let me in."

Then it was Mom and Dad's turn to exchange a look.

"You're probably wondering why we were there in the middle of the day, right?" Aaron asked.

"Actually, yes," Dad replied. "Why weren't you volunteering? And Wyatt, why weren't you at golf camp?"

I couldn't answer right away. Not until I pushed down the lump in the back of my throat with a gulp. I could feel myself on the edge of cracking, but I knew I had to trust Aaron just a little bit longer.

"Well, I left camp early that day."

"Why?" Dad asked.

"I guess I needed a break," I said. "We'd already played nine holes, and . . ."

"It was my idea," Aaron continued. "They gave all the volunteers a half day, so I texted Wyatt to see if he wanted to do something."

I wasn't sure I had one more lie in me, but I dug down deep, like I was finishing the last mile of a marathon. "We went to Pilchuck Market for chicken strips," I said, picking up the story. "It was just that one time."

"Is this the truth?" Mom asked.

"Yes," Aaron said, nodding slowly.

"Well." Dad sighed. "I can't say I like the idea of Wyatt leaving camp in the middle of the day, but I appreciate your honesty."

"In the future," Mom added, "please tell us if you do that so we know where you are."

"Can we go?" Aaron asked.

"You can set the table," Mom said, pointing to the dining room. "We're going to eat soon."

"You got it," Aaron replied.

We had dodged another bullet, but I didn't want to celebrate. At that moment, all I wanted to do was hide in my room until the Fourth of July.

"Oh, Aaron," Mom said, stirring a pot of chili on the stove. "I still haven't seen any paperwork from the parks department. And I can't seem to find any information about the volunteer program anywhere."

"Yeah," Aaron replied casually as he opened the napkin drawer. "They're not very organized. The website is way out of date. Typical city government, right, Dad?"

I began taking plates out of the cupboard, my hands shaking so much I was afraid I'd drop the whole stack.

"It's not that we don't believe you," Dad said. "It's just that we don't know anything about what you're doing."

"You should ask Wyatt what I do. He saw me a couple days ago."

Aaron didn't see it right away, but that was the moment our story finally fell apart. I just stood in the corner of the kitchen waiting for the end, not sure whether to smile or to cry.

"He did?" Mom asked.

"Yup. I think I was just finishing up lining the ball fields. So it must have been around two o'clock. Does that sound right, Wyatt?"

Dad stood in the middle of the kitchen with his arms crossed. "I'm confused. Was that the same day you stopped at Corner Pizza?"

"Huh?" Aaron said, obviously beginning to realize what he'd done.

"Wyatt said he only left golf camp early once," Dad said. "Was that the day you went to Corner Pizza or the day he saw you in the park? Or were you lying?"

Mom and Dad both looked at me. I stared right back at them, ready to face them once and for all.

"What's going on?" Mom asked. "Wyatt, did you leave golf camp early more than one time?"

Across the room, Aaron closed his eyes and swore under his breath as he realized his story had finally trapped me.

"Wyatt?" Dad said.

"I haven't been to golf camp at all," I said quietly. "I've been in the park, playing football." The words fell out of my mouth like they were being pulled by gravity.

"You've been lying to us this whole time?" Dad asked.

"I'm really sorry," I said. "I know it was wrong. But I've been playing for two weeks and I haven't gotten hurt once."

"Wyatt, this is very serious," Mom said. "You violated our trust and you put yourself at risk. What if you'd gotten hurt and we weren't able to find you? What would you have told your coach?"

"There's no coach. It's just kids."

"No coach!" Mom exclaimed. "Wyatt Parker, are you telling me the whole time we thought you were at golf camp, you've been playing unsupervised tackle football in the park without pads or helmets?"

"Yes, but it's not as bad as it sounds," I said, placing the plates on the counter. I wasn't sure which part Mom was more upset about, the tackling or the lying.

"How could it sound any worse?" Dad said, raising his voice with each word that flew out of his mouth. "You endangered yourself. You disobeyed us. And you lied to me."

"Don't yell at me," I said, feeling the internal fight in me come back. I might have been wrong to lie, but I knew on some level I had a point and I wanted to make it. "I told you I didn't want to go, but you didn't listen."

"That doesn't make it okay to lie," said Mom.

"What was I supposed to do?" I asked. "Why should I have to do whatever you guys want me to do? If you had just let me play football, we wouldn't even be having this conversation."

Aaron quietly put down the napkins and began to sneak out of the kitchen.

"Stay there!" Dad ordered, never taking his eyes off me. "Who were you playing football with, Wyatt?"

"We want to talk to their parents," Mom added.

"Friends from school?" Dad asked.

"Answer us, Wyatt," Mom insisted.

I glanced at Aaron. He was leaning against the wall. He knew he was toast. If I told Mom and Dad who I was playing with, he'd be in even more trouble.

"I'm not saying anything," I told her. "If you want to punish me, go ahead. But I'm not giving you any names. Playing football was more fun than anything I've ever done. I was good at it too. Maybe I could've gotten hurt, but it was worth the risk."

Nobody said anything.

"Also," I went on, "I think I want to try out for the high school team."

"No way, end of discussion," Mom said.

"Thanks a lot for listening," I said, making a break for the stairs.

"Wyatt!" Mom called. "Come back here!"

"Let him go," I heard Dad say.

CHAPTER TWENTY-SEVEN

I sat at my desk and stared straight ahead. I wasn't sure what to think or how to feel. For the first time in my life, I was in deep trouble. Not came-home-late-from-the-park or didn't-clean-up-my-room trouble. Serious, maximum-punishment trouble.

In some ways, I was glad it was over. When I woke up the next morning, I wouldn't have to make up a story about where I was going or where I'd been. That was a relief. But part of me was going to miss my secret life, the one where I was a football player who stood up to bullies like Spencer Randle and Julian, and who could run the wildcat better than anyone else on the field.

Thinking about that made me smile, even as I realized I was about to get grounded the day before the Fourth of July. Evan would have to watch the fireworks with her friends from the pool. When I had served my time, maybe she and I could go see *Dr. Pirate 2*. I knew she'd be up for it.

Eventually, I heard a knock on my door.

"Can I come in?" Dad asked.

"Sure," I said.

He walked into the room and sat down on my bed.

"I'm sorry I lied," I said. "And I'm sorry I played football after you told me not to."

"Thank you for saying that," Dad answered. "But that's not what's most important to me."

"Do you want me to pay you back for golf camp? Because I will."

"We'll get to that. The more important lesson is that your mom and I need you to tell us the truth, all the time, no matter what."

"I tried to," I said.

"I know you did. I should have listened. I was just really excited about playing golf with you. It's something I've been looking forward to for a long time. And now that you're finally old enough and capable, I didn't stop to think that you might not be as excited as I am. So while I can't excuse what you did, I can understand it."

"You can?"

Dad nodded. "I think you were a son so determined to do his own thing, he defied his parents." He squeezed my ankle. "But independence comes with responsibility, Wyatt. If you're going to be in charge of your own life, you have to learn to make good decisions, or there are going to be consequences."

"Can I play football again?" I asked. "There's a big game tomorrow and it's really important."

Dad was quiet for a moment.

"Can I?" I asked a minute later.

"Look, here's what's going to happen," Dad said, standing up. "Mom and I will talk tonight about what your punishment should be. Tomorrow after dinner, we'll sit down with you and Aaron and we'll let you both know what we've decided."

"Is Aaron in trouble too?"

"He lied about what he was doing. He hasn't been volunteering at all. Apparently he's just been hanging around all summer. Those were his words. So, yes, he's in trouble too. In the meantime, I'll let you judge for yourself whether playing football with your friends is the right thing to do."

"Really?" I said. I couldn't believe Dad hadn't said no. "Can I watch the fireworks too?"

Dad started to say something, then stopped himself. His expression became sad, just for a moment.

Then it seemed to pass. "I'm not saying yes or no, Wyatt. I want you to make the right decision on your own."

It wasn't until later that I realized what Dad hadn't said. But by then, there was nothing I could do.

There was a quiet moment while Dad made his way to the door. When he had one foot in the hallway, I said, "Dad?"

"Yeah?"

"I'm really sorry."

"I know you are," he replied. "But I'm not the only person you need to apologize to."

That was the understatement of the year.

The next person I had to apologize to was Mom. Then I'd have to call Francis. And Evan too, since I'd almost gotten her in trouble at the store.

As if that wasn't enough, I had no idea whether or not to play football and go to the fireworks tomorrow.

I fell asleep later that night without any clue what the right answer was. Usually I was good at multiple-choice questions, especially when there were only two options. But this one stumped me. Maybe that was because there was no right answer. If there was, I hoped I would find it in the morning.

CHAPTER TWENTY-EIGHT

The next morning I ran into Aaron in the kitchen. He was dressed in clean shorts and a collared shirt I had never seen.

"I guess you're not going to play football today," I said, pouring a glass of orange juice. "What happened?"

"They got me too," he said, cramming a toasted bagel into his mouth.

"What? How?"

"Mom and Dad aren't stupid," Aaron said, chewing as he talked. "Once they figured out you were lying, they obviously knew we were both full of it. So now I'm going down to Corner Pizza to see if Will can help me get a job."

"Where's everyone else?" I asked.

"I heard Dad and Kate split earlier this morning, and Mom is working." Aaron glanced at my clothes for the first time. "Wait a second, you're actually going to play football today? After last night?"

"Dad said it was up to me."

"Sounds like a test," said Aaron, before leaving me alone in the kitchen. "I hope you pass."

I went to the field to play football. I figured if this was the wrong decision, Dad wouldn't have given me the option to make it. He would have told me not to play.

On the way I stopped to see Francis, but nobody answered the door. It wouldn't be much longer before I realized why he wasn't home.

When I got to the field, the guys were warming up. Planet and Ox were lacing up their shoes. Shane and Julian were playing catch. And José was talking to two guys I hadn't seen before.

I walked over to José and the two new guys. "Sorry I'm late," I said.

"Oh man, Wyatt. I didn't think you were coming," José said. "I heard from your brother you guys got busted. Why are you here?"

I searched for an answer, but none came. Still thinking about the question, I reached into my backpack for a pair of socks. I jerked my hand back when my finger hit something sharp. It was a spike from my golf shoes. They had been in there all summer. Suddenly I knew what Dad hadn't said the other night—and why Francis hadn't been home this morning. They were at the father-son golf tournament, which was where I needed to be.

"I gotta go," I said to José. "I'm sorry."

José held out his hand. "Don't worry about it, wildcat. When I heard from Aaron, we called in some subs." He pointed to the two guys he'd been talking to.

"Thanks, José. I had a lot of fun playing with you."

"Right on," he said. "And hey, your brother told us you didn't say anything about the league to your parents. That was really cool. I hope you can play with us next summer. I mean, you know you'll always be an Idiot."

"Thanks. I hope I can play too."

I said goodbye to Planet, Ox, and the rest of the Idiots. Planet and Ox told me they'd look for me when school started. Then I hopped on my bike and pedaled as fast as I could to the golf course.

If I got there in time, Dad and I could still tee off in the father-son tournament. I smiled as I thought about how excited he'd be to see me. If we got lucky, maybe we'd get paired with Francis and his dad. I pedaled faster and wondered if *IE23D* was still in the theater. If I bought us two tickets, that would be a good way to say I was sorry. I bet he'd want to see it again so he could explain everything to me.

I coasted right up to the clubhouse, locked my bike, and ran inside to get my clubs. I bolted out to the first tee, but to get there, I had to pass the putting green.

Francis was there with a few other guys I didn't recognize. They were standing in a pack while one of them lined up a putt, brought his club back, and softly tapped the ball toward the hole.

"That looks like money . . . ," Francis said.

". . . in the bank!" they all said together as the ball rolled into the hole.

"Francis!" I called.

Francis told his friends he'd be right back, then came over to me. "What do you want?" he asked.

The easy answer was that I wanted everything to go back to the way it was before I had lied to Francis and ditched him at the movie theater. But I knew I couldn't just snap my fingers and change the past. Also, I wasn't even sure I really wanted everything to be exactly the way it was. Francis and I were different, and there was no rule that anyone had to have the same friends forever. That didn't mean I could just walk away, though. If we were going to go our separate ways, I had to make sure we made peace first.

"I wanted to say I'm sorry," I began. "What I did wasn't cool. I acted like a jerk. I shouldn't have lied to you, or made you lie for me, and I should have gone to see *I E Two Three-D* with you."

"Why didn't you just tell me you didn't want to go to golf camp? I would have understood."

I had a hard time believing that Francis would have understood, but I didn't think arguing with him was a good way to show I was sorry. "You're right," I said. "I should have come right out and told you. Man to man."

"Yo, Francis!" I heard his friends yell. "You're up. Are you coming?"

"So, are we cool?" I asked.

"I don't know, man," Francis answered. "Things are kind of different now. I mean, you're not the only one making new friends." Francis looked over his shoulder. "I'll be right there!" he yelled. Then he turned back to me. "Why did you come here?"

"I came to play in the tournament," I said.

"With who?"

"My dad."

"Dude, I hate to tell you this, but they teed off like an hour ago."

That didn't make sense. He couldn't be playing alone, and there was no way Aaron would have come with him. "Who was he with?"

"Kate," Francis explained. "We all watched her hit her first shot. It didn't go far, but it was straight. She's got a pretty nice swing."

"Maybe I'll just putt with you until they're done."

Francis frowned. "I don't know. I'm kind of here with these guys."

"Some other time, then," I said.

"I better go," he said. "It's hard to find five tees together. I'll see you around." Then he was gone.

I guess I had that coming, I said to myself when I was all alone. I stood on the edge of the putting green for a minute. I was waiting for something to happen, for Dad to show up and invite me to play with him and Kate, or for Francis to come back and tell me there was an open tee next to his. But that didn't happen. Hundreds of people passed by, going in all directions, but none of them had anything to say to me. Eventually I returned my bag without ever taking a club out. Then I went home.

The only sign of life in the house was the music pounding against the walls of Aaron's room. Kate and Dad wouldn't be home from the golf tournament for another few hours, and Mom was working a long shift at the hospital, probably stitching up people who forgot to throw the firecracker after lighting the fuse. Feeling an urge to tell her how I felt, I decided to write a note.

Mom,

I'm very sorry I lied to you and Dad about what I was doing this summer. I won't ever do it again. I know you think football is dangerous, but playing in the park was the first time I wasn't afraid of people who are bigger than me. Can I please try out for the freshman team? I was serious about that. If not, can I try boxing? Ha ha.

Love,
Wyatt

After leaving the note on the counter, I went next door and rang Evan's bell.

"Oh, look," she said, opening the door. "It's the criminal mastermind."

"Can we talk?" I asked, trying to show Evan that I wanted to be serious.

Apparently, I wasn't the only one not joking around.

"I'm mad at you," Evan replied, blocking the doorway. "I wasn't at first, but then I thought about what could have happened if we'd gotten caught. You know you can be arrested for shoplifting?"

"It was the dumbest thing I've ever done," I admitted. "Mostly because of what you just said. That's why I'm here to say I'm sorry. Are we still friends?"

"You're done lying and stealing?"

"I promise."

"I don't want your life of crime, Wyatt."

"You'll never see me break another law again."

Finally, Evan opened the door all the way. Now we were on her front stoop. "Anything else I should know before you're officially forgiven?"

"Well, you might not see me again for a while."

"What happened?" she asked.

"*Ka-boom,*" I said, making an explosion with my hands. "That's what."

"They found out?" Evan asked. "How?"

I told her about the scene in the kitchen and about seeing Francis at the golf club that afternoon. "Now I think I'm gonna be grounded for the rest of the summer."

"Oh man," Evan said. "Don't you get a break for being a first-time offender?"

"I don't think my parents see it that way."

"Can you at least go to the fireworks tonight?"

"It doesn't look good," I said. "Sentencing is tonight after dinner. I don't see it ending with me leaving the house."

"I'll spring you," Evan said. "I'll bring you a cupcake with a key baked inside it."

That made me laugh. I was going to miss watching the fireworks with Evan. But I knew we'd always be friends—maybe nothing more, but that was a lot better than ending up like Brian Braun and Ashley, who couldn't even hang out. I couldn't handle that. I'd already wrecked one friendship this summer.

"Thanks anyway," I said. "But I did the crime."

Evan nodded. "Gotta do the time."

"Plus, how are you going to bake cupcakes if you're up on the hill?"

"You're right," she said. "I have to get my priorities straight. Tonight is about two things. Fireworks—and fireworks." Evan kicked my ankle with her bare foot. "I wish you could go, Wyatt."

Hearing that set fireworks off in my head. It was better than actually being on the hill with her.

"If I climb on my roof, I can see them from here."

Evan stood up. "Wave to me," she said.

I waved to her.

"I mean later, dork."

"I know."

Evan stopped at the gate. "*Ka-boom,* Wyatt."

ONE MONTH LATER

Mom and Dad didn't just ground me and Aaron. They sentenced us to community service. Of course, by then all the good summer volunteer jobs were taken, so we did the only job we could find: picking up trash in the park.

"I can't believe we have to do this for another month," Aaron said one day in August after we'd been volunteering for almost three weeks. "This is worse than school."

"At least we're outside," I said.

We were sitting under the shade of a big-leaf maple tree, taking a break after work on a scorching afternoon.

Aaron wiped his brow with his wrist. "Aren't there child labor laws against this?"

"I kind of like it," I said as sweat dripped down my cheek.

"You're crazy," Aaron replied.

Maybe I was crazy. But I was also really happy. I'd done things this summer I never thought I could do, and now for the first time in my life, I had blisters, muscles, and a tan.

Too bad it wasn't from sitting by the pool.

"I'll tell you one thing," Aaron went on. "The next time I think about lying to Mom and Dad, I'm going to work a lot harder on my cover story."

"The next time?" I asked. "You'd do it again after this?" Aaron had been complaining since our first day.

"If I had to," he said. "Wouldn't you?"

"No way," I said, bouncing to my feet despite the heat and hard work. "I'm not cut out for it." Taking a swig from my water bottle, I pointed to the bathroom and told Aaron I'd see him at home.

The fields all around me were filled with kids at soccer camp and people playing Frisbee or lying in the sun. I smiled as I thought about how I'd be coming back to these fields in a few weeks—for football tryouts. Mom and Dad had signed all the permission forms just last week. Mom still didn't like it, but taking me to the sporting goods store to buy protective gear for every part of my body seemed to make her feel a little better.

I was rounding the back of the rec center on my way to the bathrooms when I heard a familiar voice.

"What's your problem, Spencer?"

"My problem is that I want some chips but I left my wallet at home."

Turning the corner, I found Francis looking up at Spencer Randle and holding a golf club. He liked to come to the field to practice with his wedge since it was closer than the driving range at the golf course.

"So go home and get it," Francis told Spencer, his voice trembling as he clutched the iron golf club in his right hand.

"Why should I go all the way home when I can just borrow the money from you?" Spencer asked, taking a step toward Francis.

Francis and Spencer were so focused on each other they hadn't noticed I was watching them. I looked around to see who else was nearby, but we were alone, blocked from view by the rec center. If anyone was going to stop what was about to happen, it was me.

I knew if I marched up to Spencer and told him to leave Francis alone, he would. But I had a feeling Francis wanted to fight his own fight.

"You want my money?" Francis asked, lifting the

club. "Come and get it. But I should warn you. I can drive a golf ball two hundred yards in the air. If I can do that, imagine what I could do to your face."

Holding up his hands, Spencer backed away. Suddenly I wasn't sure who to fight for. The League of Pain had given me the toughness to stand up for myself. After being hit like I had been, there wasn't much left to be afraid of. But the League of Pain also taught me that there could be more to other people too—and that there was more to proving myself than toughness. I decided I was going to end this business with Spencer once and for all, my way.

"What's going on?" I said innocently, coming quickly toward Spencer and Francis.

Spencer gave me a strange look. "Parker," he said. "What's up, man?"

"What's up is that you're messing with my friend," I said, standing next to Francis. "And you need to stop."

"Wyatt, I don't need your help," Francis said.

"I know," I said. "But Spencer does."

"I do?"

"Yes," I said. "If I hadn't walked by, you'd be picking your teeth out of a golf ball right now. And you're ugly enough with teeth."

"At least I don't have to stand on a dictionary to drink from the fountain," Spencer replied.

That cracked us both up.

"Wait a second," Francis said, looking at Spencer and pausing like he was trying to wrap his head around what was happening. "You know what a dictionary is?"

I wasn't sure how this would all turn out. I didn't think Spencer, Francis, and I were about to become best friends. I just had a feeling that asking for money was Spencer's messed-up way of trying to make friends. That didn't make anything he had already done right, but if I could survive the League of Pain, maybe Spencer could make it as something besides a bully. After all, like it or not, even if we weren't best friends, we all had to survive high school together. Figuring now was a pretty good time to make peace, I suggested the only thing I could think of.

"So, you guys want to go for a corn dog?"

The League of Pain
Playbook

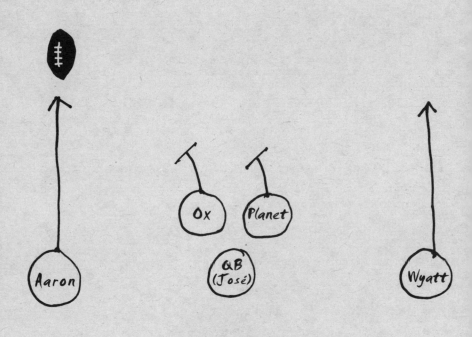

22 Falcon

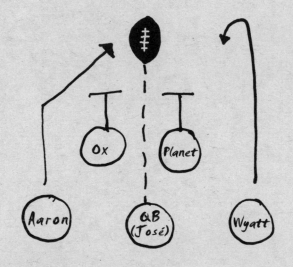

31 Eagle

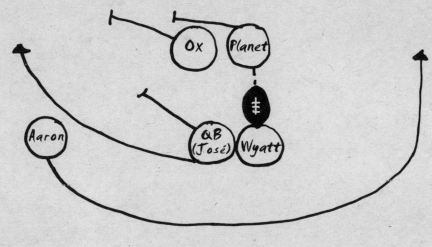

Wildcat

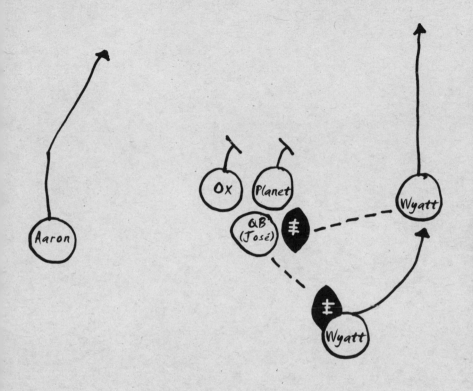

Flea-Flicker

ACKNOWLEDGMENTS

My gratitude to the old neighborhood boys for the memories and to my editor, Krista, for her hand in turning them into Wyatt's story.

ABOUT THE AUTHOR

Thatcher Heldring was born near New York City and has lived in New Jersey, South Dakota, Montana, and Washington State. When he was growing up, sports were a big part of his life, and he was pretty good at some of them. He played in plenty of tackle football games but never lied to his parents about them. He lives in Seattle with his wife, Staci, and their sons, Jack and Peter. He has read a biography of every president from George Washington to Franklin Pierce.